Comfort

Other Graphia Titles

3 NBs OF JULIAN DREW
by James M. Deem

48 SHADES OF BROWN
by Nick Earls

OWL IN LOVE
by Patrice Kindl

DUNK
by David Lubar

ZAZOO
by Richard Mosher

Check out www.graphiabooks.com

Comfort

By Carolee Dean

GRAPHIA

AN IMPRINT OF HOUGHTON MIFFLIN COMPANY
Boston

For information about permission to reproduce selections from this book,
write to Permissions, Houghton Mifflin Company,
215 Park Avenue South, New York, New York 10003.

"Kindness" from *Words Under the Words: Selected Poems* by Naomi Shihab Nye,
copyright © 1995. Used by permission of Far Corner Books,
Portland, Oregon.

www.houghtonmifflinbooks.com

Graphia and the Graphia logo are trademarks
of Houghton Mifflin Company.

The text of this book is set in Bembo.

Library of Congress Cataloging-in-Publication Data

Dean, Carolee.
Comfort / by Carolee Dean.
p. cm.
Summary: Fourteen-year-old Kenny Roy Willson fantasizes about escape from
his hometown of Comfort, Texas, following his alcoholic father's
release from prison.
(HC) ISBN 0-618-13846-3
(PB) ISBN 0-618-43912-9
[1. High schools—Fiction. 2. Schools—Fiction. 3. Poetry—Fiction. 4. Alco-
holism—Fiction. 5. Family problems—Fiction. 6. Texas—Fiction.] I. Title.
PZ7.D3435 Co 2002
[Fic]—dc21   2001039250

Manufactured in the United States of America
HAD 10 9 8 7 6 5 4 3 2 1

For my husband and partner,
Thomas Dean,
and my children,
Kristen, Jon, and Tommye Leigh

For the families of alcoholics

And in memory of Melinda McCurdy

chapter 1

I was on my way to get a hardship.

You're supposed to be at least fifteen to get a hardship driver's license but I'm not. I just turned fourteen last February. My mama dug around in the shoe box where she kept all her important papers until she found a birth certificate with my name on it, Kenny Roy Willson. Then Mama took the official document down to the library and made a Xerox copy of it. She used Wite-Out to cover up the year I was born and typed in the year before. Then she made another Xerox copy of the new birth certificate that said I was fifteen instead of fourteen.

"Ain't that a felony?" I asked her.

"Hush up, Kenny, don't worry about that," she told me.

She wouldn't be the first person in the family to commit a felony or to go to prison for it, either.

We were on our way down to the county seat over in Boerne (pronounced "Bernie") in our beat-up Chevy pickup when Mama told me, "You gotta be Daddy's driver when he comes home from the penitentiary so you can bring him to his Alcoholics Anonymous meetings over here in Boerne. They don't got AA in Comfort. Our town's too small."

"Gosh, Mama, I don't wanna do that." Daddy had racked up a total of twenty-three Driving While Intoxicated charges before robbing Smitty's Liquors and landing himself in the men's prison in Hondo. That was a record for the town of Comfort, Texas, and it didn't look likely that his driver's license would ever be reinstated in his lifetime.

"Why can't you drive him?" I asked.

"I gotta run the café," she said.

"But I got school and the paper and that University Interscholastic League contest coming up. I don't got time to drive him around."

"Don't you whine to me, boy. Your daddy's coming home next week and we all gotta pull together." We turned off on the road to the courthouse. It was rutted and hadn't been repaved for about twenty years. The suspension in the old Chevy wasn't too good and every time Mama hit a pothole, her butt flew off the seat about six inches. She had to hang onto the steering wheel with both hands just to keep herself from flying through the roof. "You can just drop that *Jackles* thing if you have to."

"*Cackles*," I said, clenching my teeth. "I ain't giving up the school paper." I had to yell because Mama was shifting down and the gears were grinding. "You already made me quit football and band to work in that stupid café." There were about six of us from the team who used to play with the band during halftime, marching in our football jerseys. "I ain't giving up the paper, no matter what you say."

"Watch your mouth." She wanted to hit me. I could see it in her eyes as they darted around the cab of the truck looking for something to use to whack me.

Mama had made me quit the football team even though I was the only freshman to ever make varsity. Even after Coach Billings made a special trip down to the café to tell her how much the team needed me. I wasn't big in size but I was fast and I could catch a ball.

Then Viola Wambat begged her to at least let me stay in the band. But Mama didn't give an inch. She never did. Now all I could do was write about other kids' achievements in the school paper. It was all I had and I wasn't giving it up for any drunk. "I wish Daddy would just stay in prison," I said without thinking.

One hand flew off the wheel as she reached for a rolled-up newspaper, but then she lost her bearings, hit a pothole, and bumped her head on the roof of the truck just as we pulled into a parking space next to a line of police cars.

I jumped out before Mama could get a hold of me. She bounced out of the truck and rolled toward me like a steam engine. She was twice my size around and one heck of a lot meaner.

"Morning," said a policeman, leaning on his patrol car and writing on a clipboard.

Mama shut down her internal engines and smiled at the man. "Morning, officer." I guess she didn't want to plow me down right there in front of the law because instead of screaming like she usually did, she grabbed my arm and whispered in my ear. "Your daddy's gonna make something of himself in that café. I got dreams and plans and I'm giving you notice, you better do what I say." With that, she dragged me off toward the courthouse.

I had dreams of my own.

They did not include my mama, the café, a snot-nosed baby brother, or a no-account drunk daddy.

The way I saw it, they were my real hardship.

chapter 2

Daddy came home from prison in late January. Mama threw a Welcome Home Roy Party a week later, but nobody attended except for me, Mama, Roy junior (my three-year-old baby brother), and Jake, the local sheriff who used to be Daddy's best friend before Roy senior turned to a life of crime. Mama and Daddy and Jake went to high school together. The story goes that Jake was sweet on Mama until my daddy stole her away with his guitar and his sweet talk and all the songs he wrote for her. Sometimes I imagine that Jake's my real father, and he's just too polite to let on about it. He took good care of us while Daddy was away. He made sure I always had a jacket for the winter and a little change in my pocket. He didn't come around as much after Daddy got back. I wished he was around more and my daddy was around less.

I had always been afraid of Daddy. It wasn't that he was a violent man. He'd never actually laid a hand on me. It was just that he had so much anger and disappointment simmering below the surface that I was never sure of what he might do.

That night Mama made us all start wearing "Roy's Place" T-shirts. She wore hers knotted around her waist over a black spandex skirt that was two sizes too small. With her black leather boots, she looked like she should be on the back of a Harley.

I wore mine under a flannel shirt that was buttoned to the collar.

I shouldn't say nobody else came to the party, because Todd Anderson, R.J. Rice, and Petey Simpson, three seniors from the football team, stopped by the café for about thirty seconds.

"Where's the beer?" asked Todd when my mama was out of earshot. Todd was a defensive tackle. His massive arms hung from his shoulders like two huge sausage links. I wrote a story about him after the homecoming game this past season. He'd sacked the quarterback five times and I referred to him as "the Steam Roller of Comfort High." After that, Cindy Blackwell, the prettiest girl in the history of south central Texas, started going with Todd. Maybe he figured it was because of the article I wrote or maybe he just liked what I said about him, but anyway, he and the guys started catering to me pretty regular.

"We don't got any beer, just Pepsi Cola," I told Todd.

"You don't have any beer!" Petey howled.

"I thought your daddy was a drunk," said Todd, gulping his Pepsi. Then he stuck his face down into the plate and sucked up a mouthful of chips. He had what the girls referred to as a "prehensile lip." It was like watching a horse eat oats off the ground. A miserable thing to witness.

Mama looked across the café at the boys and gave them the eye.

I whispered. "He's in Alcoholics Anonymous now. He can't drink."

"That's the dangdest thing I ever heard," said Petey, stuffing his pockets full of pretzels.

Daddy sat over in the corner talking to Jake and tuning his guitar. Daddy wore a pair of faded jeans and an old flannel shirt. Everything about him looked softer and more worn than it had when he left, especially the shoots of gray in his chestnut brown hair. I hoped he'd gotten softer in prison and not harder, but only time would tell.

Todd stared at him as if he was some kind of deviant, a drunk who didn't drink.

Mama noticed Todd eyeing Daddy and I could tell she didn't like it none. Mama came out from behind the counter carrying a bowl of chips in one arm and Roy junior in the other. In my opinion the child was too big to be carried around, but if she wasn't carrying him, the kid tugged on her skirt and slowed her down. I also thought he was too big to be wearing diapers and drinking out of a bottle. In fact, I thought he was too big and fat in general.

Mama banged the bowl of chips down on the table

so hard that we all jumped. "You boys ready to hear Roy sing?"

"No, ma'am. Actually, we were about to go," said Todd.

"Hmpf," said Mama, blowing her bangs out of her face and stomping back behind the counter with Roy junior in tow. "Hmpf," said Roy junior, blowing his bangs, then taking a bite out of a chocolate bar. The kid was a chocolate junkie. He'd go on a chocolate binge and eat the stuff until he puked. What he couldn't eat, he hid. I considered that a bad sign, considering our family history of compulsive behavior. But nobody asked for my opinion, so I kept it to myself.

Daddy's singing was a matter Mama took very seriously. She'd taken every dime we made out of the café and put it into music equipment—a brand-new guitar, amplifiers, recording equipment, and lights. She even made me spend all of Christmas vacation building a stage over in a corner of the restaurant. I missed the Christmas parade and everything.

I barely had a spare minute to practice for the UIL journalism and poetry events, but I made time. It was the only thing that kept me focused.

Todd went back to staring at Daddy. "Don't keep looking at him as if he was some kind of anomaly," I said.

"Anoma what?" asked Todd.

"An abnormality." I like to try out new words every now and then because Mrs. Peterson, my English teacher and the sponsor for the school paper, says that words give you power. They can take you places you never thought possible. I also have what I call my "home" language and my "school" language. I used to try practicing proper grammar at home, but Mama kept saying, "Something's wrong with you, Kenny, I just can't figure out what, but you sound funny to me."

"It ain't so unusual for a person to abstain," I told them. "You might consider giving it a try."

Petey looked at me as if I was from Mars. "Why?"

"My aunt Trudy's been to AA," said R.J. "They just sat around drinking coffee and smoking cigarettes. She has asthma so she figured she'd be safer back on the bourbon."

Petey grabbed a handful of chips. "If there's one person in Comfort with a worse reputation than your daddy, Kenny, it would be R.J.'s aunt."

R.J. beamed with family pride. "One time she met this guy and married him while she was in an alcohol-induced blackout. She came to and found him in her bed and thinking he was a prowler she shot him in the leg. The man had the marriage annulled and Judge Billings gave Trudy the choice of a rehabilitation hospital or jail. She chose jail."

"What's the worst thing your daddy ever done?" challenged Petey.

"I heard he killed a guy in prison," said Todd.

I felt my stomach turning. There was a rumor that Daddy had killed a man in prison but the officials couldn't prove he'd done it. I didn't know where the rumor started. I didn't want to know. "Why ain't Cindy with you?" I asked Todd, trying to change the subject.

Todd's huge fist suddenly flew out toward my neck. He grabbed my collar, choking me, and pulled my face close to his.

"What did you say?" he hollered. He might have been playing with me. He sometimes did that with his "friends," but you could never be sure with Todd. All the same, I couldn't breathe.

"Where's Cindy?" my voice was raspy because hardly any air was coming out of my mouth.

"Don't let me ever hear you say my woman's name again."

"Your woman," laughed Petey. "I thought she dumped you."

Todd let go of my collar and I took in a long gulp of air. He took a fistful of potato chips and shoved them down Petey's shirt.

"Women don't dump me," said Todd. "They have momentary lapses in sanity which cause them to become overwhelmed by my presence. They might take a time-out, but they never call game. They always come back around."

"I don't know," said R.J. "She sounded pretty sane when she called you a two-faced, lying, cheating swine."

"She'll come back around. That girl is mine."

I didn't like the way Todd said it, as if she was a boot or a car.

"Come on, boys, let's get outta here," Todd said to R.J. and Petey. They crammed their pockets full of food, then strutted out the front door, punching each other in the ribs. I watched them through the window as they piled into Petey's Toyota pickup. Those three huge monsters looked like sardines hanging out the sides of a can.

"I don't like those boys," said Mama. "They're trouble."

They may have been trouble, but I envied them just the same. They were free to come and go, free to cruise the highway, free to play football on Friday night.

All I could do was sit at the café and see the lights from the field down the highway and hear the soft roar of the crowd in the background. Then I'd think about how it used to feel to be smack-dab in the middle of that roar. At school I was somebody even if I was on the free lunch program and had holes in my jeans.

At the café I was just a kid who couldn't do anything right.

Daddy finished tuning his guitar. Mama turned the overhead lights down low and fixed a spotlight on Daddy. Jake came over and sat next to Roy junior and me.

Then Mama went up on the stage and hugged Daddy's neck and cried. "It's good to have you home, baby."

Then Daddy cried. "Maggie, I ain't never gonna let you

down again, honey, I swear it." Then they kissed. Roy junior clapped and ate another chocolate bar.

"I think I'm gonna puke," I told Jake.

He smiled. "Just let 'em have some time."

Mama came and sat down next to me. Daddy turned on the microphone and it squealed until he adjusted it. "I'd like to dedicate this first song to my lovely wife, the love of my life, Maggie Willson."

Then Daddy sang and Roy junior got up onstage and danced wearing nothing but a diaper and cowboy boots. Big fat tears continued to roll down Mama's cheeks and she had to blow her nose with a paper napkin. My nausea returned. When Daddy finished his song Mama clapped until I thought her hands would fly off the ends of her arms. Then she reached over and squeezed my hand. "Your daddy's gonna be the best country-and-western singer that ever lived. He's gonna go all the way to the top and we're gonna help him make it happen."

Like all of Mama's schemes, that just sounded too good to be true. Especially considering the catastrophe that occurred when Daddy tried to play at the Kerrville Folk Festival nearly four years earlier. It had started with too much to drink and ended with him in prison.

My fifteenth birthday came a week later, on February 12. I didn't get a party. Mama didn't remember. The next day she handed me a package. "Take this down to the post office and mail it and don't breathe a word about this to your daddy." It was a box stuffed inside a big brown envelope addressed to Starlite Records in Nashville, Tennessee.

Mama's scheming had begun. I felt as if I was on a roller coaster. I could sense disaster up ahead, but I had no way to get off. All I could do was close my eyes, hang on tight, and hope I survived the ride.

chapter 3

I wiped down the counter while Mama busied herself off in the back with the tapes returned from record producers in Nashville. So far not one of them had recognized the vocal talents of Roy Dan Willson, and it was driving Mama crazy. It had only been two weeks and already everything Mama had sent out had been returned. I wondered if anybody ever listened to the tapes or if they just sent them back as soon as they arrived.

Mama muttered under her breath as she put new mailing labels on the brown envelopes and got ready to send them out again. "No ear for talent," she said half a dozen times. "I don't understand it," Mama droned as she hid the extra tapes behind the dishwashing soap. It was a place Daddy was sure never to look. "They come back so fast. It just ain't logistical."

"Do you mean it ain't 'logical'?" I said, doubting that she was talking about the logistics of mailing items between Nashville and Comfort.

Mama shoved a mop bucket at me. "I meant whatever I said, and I said whatever I meant. Now go clean the floor in the dining room."

I carried the bucket out front and started mopping from one side of the dining room to the other, wondering how I'd ever find the time to prepare for the poetry competition.

Mrs. Peterson says words have power. If that's true then the most potent thing in my life during that time when Daddy first got home was the word "Dallas."

That's where I was going. I wasn't stupid about it, though. I watched the news and *Sixty Minutes*. I knew what happened to runaways out on the streets. I wasn't going to be out on the streets. I had a plan. And I wasn't running away. I was merely going to relocate prematurely. The mistake most kids make is that they fly off the handle and get scared or mad at their parents and just take off from home without thinking about it ahead of time. Not me. I'd been thinking about leaving for a long time.

The idea started that freshman year in early October, the day Mama pulled me off the football team to slave my youth away in that stupid café—scrubbing floors, cleaning the fryer, waiting on customers. I asked Mama how much she was going to pay me to work my rear off like a dog. She grabbed a newspaper and whacked me in the mouth.

"Talk like a dog, get whooped like a dog," she'd said. Mama didn't tolerate lip of any kind. "We're a family and we pull together. You'll do your part, Kenny, and you won't talk back to me about it."

That's right. I'll keep my mouth shut. But Mama, one day you'll wake up and I won't be here for you to push around.

The thing about Mama was that she could be whacking you one minute and hugging you the next. She didn't mean anything by hitting me. It was just her way of expressing her irritation. But it hurt just the same. I wondered if she ever considered my feelings. I wondered if she had any hint of how I sometimes wanted to rip her head off, and how much the feeling scared me.

After that discussion I decided that salary negotiations would have to go on the back burner. But I also knew I wasn't going to work for free. I started by taking five dollars a week from the cash register, then I eased my way up to ten. Mama had me doing the books so I just logged my "salary" in under miscellaneous expenses. I knew Mama would never check out the financial records. She had a habit of not looking at things she didn't want to see. The simple truth was that the café was losing money.

Mama wasn't a bookkeeper. For that matter she wasn't a cook or even much of a waitress. It was still unclear to me why she'd bought the café.

At first I felt guilty about reallocating money from the restaurant toward my "Dallas Fund," but then I figured my mama was violating all kinds of child labor laws by working me as hard as she did. I eased up to twenty a week. When I calculated that the amount still totaled less than a dollar an hour for hard labor, I didn't feel bad about it anymore. It had become a matter of self-preservation. After saving my cut for over four months, I had almost four hundred dollars tucked away in a shoe box under my bed. My goal was one thousand by the time school got out for the summer. Then I'd be history. With a thousand dollars in my pocket I could catch a bus to Dallas, rent an efficiency apartment, and find some kind of job. I could work on getting my GED, then start school at the vocational institute and learn a trade.

I'd have another two or three hundred saved from my "earnings" at the café, but that wouldn't be enough. The key was the UIL competition.

I was signed up for three events: newswriting, sportswriting, and poetry interpretation. The UIL didn't give out cash prizes. It was a violation of their rules, but the local Lion's Club did. I guess it was to encourage kids to get involved. It sure encouraged me when I found out about it. Any kid from Comfort who went to the state finals and won first place in any category got a check for five hundred dollars. Second place was three hundred dollars and third place was one hundred. If I won first or second place in any event at the state level, I'd be sitting pretty.

I'd be free.

And while I was in Dallas, I could try to find Grandpa Harris. He was Mama's daddy and the only sane adult from either side of the family. I'd only actually met him once. When I was eight years old he took me out for a hot dog. He was funny and I could tell by his immaculate white loafers that he had class.

Cindy Blackwell walked up behind me as I was finishing the floor and kissed the top of my head. She was a senior and a good five inches taller so she looked down on me and I guess the top of my head held some kind of appeal, because she had a habit of kissing it, as if I was a puppy or her little brother. "Hey kid," she said. "Fix me a malt, would you?"

My first reaction was to jerk my head around in a three-hundred-and-sixty-degree radius and make sure her boyfriend, Todd Anderson, wasn't around. I lived in mortal fear that one day he would witness her planting her lips on the top of my head and he'd use his big, meat loaf hands to separate my face from my skull. I'd seen him pulverize guys for lesser offenses. But there was nobody in the front of the café but Cindy and me.

"No taste in music," I heard Mama yell from the back as I scooped the ice cream and put it in the blender. I added some milk and a scoop of malt, then I carried the concoction as I followed Cindy over to a table. She was toting a thick black book. I tried to keep my eyes fixed on her short, bouncy, dark brown hair to avoid looking at the other parts of her, like her legs, which stretched from Texas to Missouri. She was tall and lithe and she moved like a dancer even though she had stopped taking ballet when she was eight.

The one thing even remotely holding me to the town of

Comfort was Cindy Blackwell. If I could have just figured out a way to fit the name "Cindy" into the same sentence with the word "Dallas," I might have died and gone to heaven.

Cindy sat down, put the book on the seat, and licked the ice cream that was dripping down the side of the container. I watched her tongue scoop up the cream as it made a little stream down the frosty exterior of the metal cup. I sat down across from her and handed her a napkin, but she waved it away.

"You better be careful," I said.

"Why?"

"'Cause your tongue is gonna stick to the side of the metal cup."

"Oh." She scooped up the rest with her pinky, then licked it off her finger.

"Sally's not speaking to me," said Cindy, swirling the malt with a spoon. Sally Mayer was Cindy's best friend, but I didn't know why because she stayed mad at Cindy most of the time.

"And I broke up with Todd again." She looked sad.

"Yeah?" I said, trying not to sound too interested.

"I don't understand him. He can be so nice one minute and such a Neanderthal the next. Besides, I'm too busy for dating right now." She smiled and perked up. "I've got to get ready for the UIL competition. Have you picked your poems?"

"I'm working on it," I lied. I hadn't even had time to think about it.

Cindy was hooked on poetry and she'd talked me into signing up for the poetry-interpretation portion of the University Interscholastic League competition, in addition to the newswriting and sportswriting events for which I had already been preparing. The UIL competition in Johnson City in two weeks was the only thing I had to look forward to in my sorry life. It meant a whole day with Cindy away from the café and away from Todd's watchful eyes.

Cindy grabbed the book sitting next to her and set it on the table. It was thick and smelled of mildew. Cindy's eyes lit up as she opened to a page in the middle. "Here's the poem I read last year when I won second place at district, 'Invictus' by William Ernest Henley. You can use it if you want." She closed her eyes and recited from memory quite dramatically. The words didn't so much flow as explode out of her:

> Out of the night that covers me,
> Black as the Pit from pole to pole,
> I thank whatever gods may be
> For my unconquerable soul.

She opened her eyes and pushed the book toward me. "Here, try it."

But I couldn't speak. I sat in awe. Cindy had made those

lines vibrate with life. "I don't know," I stalled. I didn't want to try reciting something in front of her. "Ain't Henley some dead English dude? Don't we have to pick pieces that were written by multicultural poets like Maya Angelou?"

"The category is Diversity and the Human Experience," Cindy corrected me. "Maya Angelou would be good but so would Henley. Remember, you have to have several pieces and you're supposed to look beyond the obvious experience of ethnicity. There are all kinds of different people in the world, with all different types of struggles."

"This is starting to sound complicated," I said, wondering if I'd ever be ready in time for the competition.

"What makes Maya Angelou's poems powerful? Is it just because she's black or because of her other life experiences? When she writes about a caged bird, you know she understands what it means to be caged."

"I never thought about it like that," I said.

Cindy stirred her malt slowly and thoughtfully. "The poet is the poem, Kenny. That's the only thing that gives the words any meaning. You have to feel that in your soul."

"I don't know," I said.

Cindy leaned across the table toward me and her eyes lit up with excitement. "Did you know that Henley had one of his legs amputated when he was a kid?"

"That's terrible," I said, thinking about how much I loved to run when I was on the football team.

"Then when he was twenty-four his doctor told him the other leg had to come off too."

"Both legs?"

"They ended up saving the leg but he was in the hospital for nearly two years. That's when he wrote 'Invictus.'"

"Wow" was all I could think to say.

"So you could use Henley for Diversity and the Human Experience, or the other category, Words of Inspiration."

"What other category?" I asked, feeling a sudden panic come over me.

"You have to prepare two separate performances," she said, finishing the last of her malt.

"Two!" I hadn't even started preparing for one. "Why two?"

"That's just the way they do it."

"This sounds like a lot more work than the sportswriting contest," I said, wondering if there was any way to back out of it.

Cindy winked at me. "Yeah, but it will be worth it." I thought I saw a glint of promise in her eyes.

She pushed the book closer to me. "Go on. Give it a try."

I looked at the page and tried to speak but the words got caught down in my throat. "I can't do it like you did," I finally muttered.

"Just try," she smiled.

I coughed to clear my throat and my head. Then I read:

> *In the fell clutch of circumstance*
> *I have not winced nor cried aloud.*
> *Under the bludgeonings of chance*
> *My head is bloody, but unbowed.*

"No, not like that," said Cindy. "Don't read it as if you were reciting a grocery list." She jumped out of her seat and hopped up on Daddy's stage right next to his guitar.

> *Beyond this place of wrath and tears*
> *Looms but the horror of the shade,*
> *And yet the menace of the years*
> *Finds, and shall find me, unafraid.*

> *It matters not how strait the gate,*
> *How charged with punishments the scroll,*
> *I am the master of my fate:*
> *I am the captain of my soul.*

Every word seemed to gush out of her mouth like a raging river. I stopped breathing. I didn't want to miss one syllable or vowel.

I knew Cindy would make it out of Comfort. She was the jewel of the school. The one voted most likely to blaze her own trail. I prayed that I would make it out, too.

"What do you think you're doing?" I heard Mama's shrill voice call to Cindy from the other side of the café.

Cindy opened her eyes and took a step backward, knocking over Daddy's music stand. "I was just reciting a poem."

Mama ran across the café and picked up the stand, dusting it off and setting it upright. "Get down from there," she yelled at Cindy. "This ain't no place for kids. Get down before you break something."

Cindy stepped down from the stage looking like a kicked dog. I wanted to wring Mama's neck.

Cindy sat down across from me and fixed her eyes on the empty malt container. Mama dusted off the guitar and made a point of inspecting it right there in front of Cindy.

"Kenny, you keep your friends away from Daddy's stuff."

"Yes, ma'am," I said. I wanted to tell her to go jump in the deep fryer, but I'd learned long ago not to start battles I had no chance of winning.

"And get back to work. This ain't break time."

Mama stormed back off into the kitchen. As soon as she was out of earshot, Cindy's eyes lit back up and she giggled uncontrollably. "I believe your Mama might just be meaner than my Daddy."

I laughed, too. Buddy Blackwell, ex-marine, ex-weight lifter, had a reputation for being a hothead. "If not, she's a close second," I said.

She leaned across the table and lowered her voice to a whisper. "You ever been to a slam?" she asked.

"What's a slam?" I asked.

"Kenny, get your butt back in this kitchen right this minute!" yelled Mama.

"Meet me out back at midnight this Saturday," whispered Cindy.

"Okay," I said, knowing perfectly well that Mama wouldn't let me go anywhere with anybody on Saturday night.

Cindy stood up. "And keep the poem. Maybe you can use it for the contest."

"Thanks," I called to Cindy as she left. I tucked the book under my arm and went back to the kitchen, wondering where to hide it. Every little thing seemed to irritate Mama lately, and I didn't want her to trip over the book and get crossways about me going to Johnson City.

I smiled to myself. The prettiest girl in the history of the town had just asked me to go out with her. Getting away from the café on a Saturday night seemed impossible, but I would find a way.

chapter 4

The next day was Monday. I drifted through my classes, then I spent the rest of the afternoon daydreaming about Cindy. Mama kept asking me why I was smiling so much. It seemed to bother her.

"What has gotten into you?" she said as I finished mopping.

I'd been whistling. I pointed to the shining floor and replied, "Nothing, Mama. I'm just rapturously overjoyed by the delightful gratification of a task finalized to satisfaction."

Mama hated it when I used words she didn't know. She narrowed her eyes and said, "I think you read too much."

I hurried into the kitchen with my mop bucket so Mama wouldn't see me laughing.

She came around the corner a couple of minutes later. "Girl's looking for you," she said in irritation.

I hurried up front, hoping it was Cindy.

"Don't take long, you got work," said Mama on her way to the freezer.

But when I got to the front counter I saw that it wasn't Cindy. It was just her short scrawny sister Suzie with a camera around her neck. She'd been wearing it ever since she got on the yearbook committee.

"Hi, Kenny," she smiled.

"Hi, Suzie. What do you need?"

Suzie wore her long, stringy blonde hair in a ponytail to keep it out of her eyes because she probably couldn't figure out anything more attractive to do with it. She was a freshman, too, but to me she seemed a lot younger. Suzie was a track star with the fastest time for the hurdle race in the history of Comfort High and everybody thought she was really something. She still wore that fresh-glazed, excited look of someone who thinks they are somebody before they realize they're nobody. I had that look when I used to play football.

"Have you seen Cindy?" she asked.

"Not since yesterday," I said, looking like I had to tend to more important things.

"Okay." She seemed disappointed, and when I started to arrange a few things on the counter, she said "Thanks anyway" and left.

Todd and the guys always called her Shadow because she followed Cindy around like a little puppy dog. Cindy was nice about it. She usually let her tag along. It was a big deal for a freshman to be let into the upper classmen's crowd. I knew because they'd let me in when I played football and I'd kind of stayed.

I couldn't really blame Suzie. I'd sure follow Cindy all over town if I could.

The phone rang and Mama came up front to answer it. "Hello, Roy's Place. Featuring nightly the talents of Roy Dan Willson, the best darn country-and-western singer this side of Memphis.

"Uh-huh," she continued after a short pause. "A job interview at the lumberyard? I'm sure he'd appreciate that, but he's already taken another job. . . . Okay. Thank you. Bye."

"What other job?" I asked.

"Hush," said Mama. "Your daddy's coming."

Daddy walked into the café carrying Roy junior just as Mama hung up the phone. He put Roy junior on the floor and the kid made a beeline for the doughnut display. I gave him a doughnut and he licked off the chocolate frosting, then tried to hand me the remains. "Here, Kenny. Want a cookie?"

Everything was a cookie—the doughnuts, the honey buns, the Twinkies.

"No thanks, kid. I'm trying to cut down."

Roy junior shrugged his shoulders and put the half-eaten doughnut on the floor.

"Who was that on the phone?" Daddy asked Mama.

"Salesman," she said, looking away guiltily.

"Thought it might be somebody calling me back about a job. I put in at least twenty applications around town."

"Something will come up, baby." Mama wiped the counter

to avoid looking him in the eye. I wondered who was more dishonest, Mama or Daddy. I remembered how Daddy was before they hauled him off to prison. He'd say the sky was green just to see who might believe him.

"I talked to Hank at the lumberyard a week ago. He said he thought he had a place for me. Maybe I should just give him a call."

Daddy reached for the phone.

"No!" Mama yelled. Daddy and I both looked at her.

"What's wrong?" asked Daddy.

"I forgot. He called yesterday. Said they already found somebody."

Daddy put down the phone, sat on a barstool, and shook his head. He looked beat up. "They found somebody *else,* in other words. Somebody who ain't an ex-con."

Mama put the rag down, walked up behind him, put her arms around him, and rocked him like a child. "Don't take it like that, baby. You got a job here, singing."

Daddy's face turned bright red. I couldn't tell if he was angry or embarrassed. He pounded his fist on the counter, sending pepper shakers and ketchup bottles dancing. Mama and I jumped back in surprise. Good thing there were no patrons in the café.

Roy junior grabbed onto my leg and looked up at me with frightened eyes. I scooped him up and diverted his attention to the counter. "Want another cookie?" I asked him as I lifted the glass cover from the doughnut display. He gave me a big smile and picked up another chocolate doughnut. I carried him into the kitchen.

I could still hear Daddy's agitated voice. "I don't wanna be a kept man, Maggie," he said angrily.

Roy junior buried his head in my chest and got chocolate icing all over my shirt, but I didn't say anything about it. I guess I felt sorry for the kid.

"It's gonna be okay," I told him, but I wasn't so sure. Daddy was jumpy since coming back from prison, on edge, unpredictable.

"Why don't you let me do some real work around here. I'm tired of changing diapers," he yelled.

Roy junior looked down self-consciously at his pants.

"I don't want you to get tired. You gotta save your energy to sing. That's your job. That's what brings in the customers," said Mama.

"I ain't bringing in any customers, Maggie, or ain't you noticed." His voice suddenly quieted. "Why can't you just admit the truth? You don't trust me."

"No, that ain't it, baby. How can you talk like that? You know you mean the world to me. Everything I do, I do for you." Mama was crying. I could hear it in her voice.

"I'm sick and tired of sitting around, waiting for my life to start. You got any idea what that does to a man?"

I had a pretty good idea. That's exactly how I'd spent the last three, nearly four years.

Suddenly I heard the bells on the front door jingle as it opened and slammed shut.

Mama came running into the kitchen. "He took the keys to the truck. He ain't supposed to drive," Mama said, frantically grabbing Roy junior out of my arms. "Go out after him."

"Me?" The last thing I wanted was to be with my daddy in his state of mind.

"You want him to get thrown back in jail?" she screamed. Her face puffed out as if she would explode and the veins stuck out in her neck.

"Kenny!" Roy junior was reaching for me, trying to get away from Mama. She set him in his playpen.

I realized my choices were to stay with my crazy mama or go out after my crazy daddy. Roy junior looked at me with pleading eyes through the nylon mesh of his prison.

"Sorry kid," I told him as I ran out of the kitchen. I felt as if I'd just deserted a wounded soldier on the battlefield, but I figured Mama would quit carrying on if I did what she told me.

I found Daddy sitting out front in the pickup, the engine running, his head resting on the steering wheel.

"Daddy, Mama says I'm supposed to drive you."

"Why?" he asked without looking up.

"So you don't get thrown back in jail for violating your parole."

"Go on back inside."

"No, sir. I can't do that. Mama says —"

He looked up from the steering wheel and yelled, "I don't care what Mama says. Don't nobody around here give a dang what I say?"

Who are you to yell at me? You're nothing but a stinking ex-con drunk. But I couldn't call him that to his face.

"Daddy, it's been three years since you went off to prison. Things are different now. Mama's gonna whoop me good if I don't drive you. She got mean since you been gone."

I expected him to unload and tell me what he'd do if I didn't listen to him, but he didn't. His eyes got very sad. I never realized how blue and soft they were. Mama had said many times that she fell in love with Daddy because of his voice, but she married him because of his eyes. Just then I understood what she meant. He seemed to look right through me, as if he understood. He opened the door and then he scooted over to the passenger seat. "Get in."

I got in behind the wheel. "Where to?"

"Smitty's."

My palms grew wet and cold and I froze. I noticed a white envelope sitting on the seat between us. It was bulging with twenty-dollar bills. I didn't know where it came from, but it was pretty clear where it was going.

Driving to Smitty's Liquors would be like buying a one-way ticket to the electric chair.

"Put it in gear," said Daddy, "or else get out and let me drive myself."

If I went back inside, Mama would throw a fit. At least with me driving, Daddy wouldn't get in a car wreck if he got drunk. I didn't know what else to do, so I put the truck in gear and drove south toward Highway 27. It was the highway that led toward Kerrville, toward Smitty's, and toward disaster.

chapter 5

We passed the antique shops and historic houses on High Street, then we crossed over Cypress Creek. One-hundred-year-old cottonwood trees and cypresses lined the banks. All the foliage of the Texas hill country had turned a deep green due to the recent rains.

I turned onto Highway 27. I use the term "highway" loosely. It was more like a wide clearing through the vegetation. The nearer I got to Smitty's, the slower I drove. I could smell German sausages cooking at the Smokehaus Sausage Palace and it reminded me I hadn't eaten lunch. Mr. Lowenstein, the owner, sat out on the porch playing his concertina for the customers. He did that when things got slow.

Next door I saw Mrs. Hodge tacking up a sign in front of the Comfort Emporium that read, "Everything Half Price." Mrs. Hodge was about ninety years old and she had accumulated ninety years' worth of junk. When her husband was alive he had to build an extra room on the house to store it all in. Then he died and she moved in with her son. He wouldn't let her store her "collectibles" with him so she opened up the Emporium and kept it all there. I don't think she ever sold anything. It was more like a museum dedicated to trash.

"You drive like an old lady, Kenny. Step on the gas," said Daddy.

I reluctantly drove a little further down that two-lane highway that ran through the center of town and parked across the street from the liquor store, hoping it wouldn't be too obvious where we were heading. We were about a half-mile from the county line. A sign that read "To Kerrville" kept staring me in the face.

Memorial Day weekend three and a half years earlier was the last time Daddy got drunk. He was supposed to play at the Kerrville Folk Festival. Mama was pregnant with Roy junior and sick as a dog. I was eleven at the time. Daddy had lost his trucker job and the utility bills were all overdue. Mama got it in her head that if Daddy could win first prize at the festival we could have the electricity reconnected. And maybe Daddy would get discovered. She'd sent in a demo tape and the festival committee had called him in for an audition. That went okay, but as the day of the actual performance drew closer, Daddy got nervous. Then he got mean and spiteful. One day he ran over my bicycle with his truck because he said I left it in his way, which didn't make any sense, because I'd left it on the sidewalk.

Mama grew sicker and went into the hospital, leaving me alone with Daddy. I was scared. Then they said she might die, or the baby might die, or they both might die, and I got even more scared. Daddy fell apart. He started drinking even more to calm his nerves. He drank so much I thought he'd pickle himself. I cooked canned soup for every meal because that was all we had. Daddy never ate unless I reminded him.

The day he got up onstage in Kerrville in front of all those people, he stumbled around and the crowd started laughing. He ran out, drove to Smitty's, and robbed the liquor store.

I'll never forget the evening when Jake came over to the house. It was a hot, humid June night and we didn't have any air-conditioning or any food in the icebox because the utility company had turned off the electricity. I was hungry and alone because Daddy hadn't come back from Kerrville. I'd been alone a lot since Mama had gone into the hospital.

Jake said, "Your mama's still real sick and your daddy's in jail. You're gonna stay with me for a while."

I was relieved. I wanted to stay with him forever.

Jake reminded me of Grandpa Harris. They both had huge guts and deep laughs that seemed to shake their entire bodies from the inside out.

———

Daddy and I sat out in front of Smitty's for a good thirty minutes before either of us said a word. Daddy looked across the street at the store, then he reached for the truck handle. He started to open the door, then he shut it before getting out. My mind was working the whole thing over. If I brought him back to Mama drunk I might as well grab my money box and make a beeline for Dallas. I sure could use that extra bundle of cash Daddy had on the seat next to him. If I had that money I wouldn't have to hang around for the UIL. I could leave immediately. But then Daddy would drive home drunk and probably kill somebody and Mama would fall apart. Then Roy junior would be left without any parents. I put the idea out of my head and tried to figure out how to stop Daddy.

But if his mind was set on drinking, I couldn't prevent him. Still, I had to try.

"Daddy, if I bring you back drunk, Mama will kill me. Then she'll whoop me, then she'll kill me again."

He didn't seem to hear. He grabbed the envelope full of money, jumped out of the truck, and walked across the street. He got about halfway, then he stopped and kicked the blacktop in frustration, and just stood there with traffic passing him by on both sides. Finally he turned and walked back toward the truck.

I was relieved.

He sat in the passenger seat and buried his face in his hands. Then he looked at the store again and let out a groan. "Dang, I can't do it."

I let myself take a deep breath and realized I hadn't been breathing much since taking the wheel.

"Head on down the highway."

I obeyed. I had no idea where we were going or why. I was just glad to be leaving Smitty's.

"Turn left up ahead," he said just before the county line. I turned left, drove about another mile, and found myself in front of the Comfort Junkyard. It was actually a transfer station where trash sat around waiting to be carried off somewhere else, but we all called it the junkyard.

Daddy hopped out of the truck. He opened the gate, which wasn't locked, and walked inside. I wondered what he was doing and thought it best to keep my distance and watch from the pickup. He started throwing stuff. Whatever he could lay his hands on. Old tires, sinks, broken chairs. He picked up something that looked like a huge, striped candy cane. I guessed it was the leg of an old swing set. He set a glass bottle on the hood of some old, dilapidated Chevy and *whack,* he knocked it into the outfield, sending glass flying. Then he hit another, and another. At first his anger scared me. Then it became almost poetic to watch.

Whack! He sent a beer bottle flying so high I thought it would land in Johnson City. My fingers twitched. I had it in me to go out there with him and bust up some stuff of my own. Every time he hit a bottle, I felt my hands tighten around the steering wheel, but I couldn't build up the nerve to move from where I was sitting. I had anger in me itching to get out, but I feared that if I ever opened that door, I wouldn't be able to shut it.

Daddy worked himself into exhaustion, leaned the swing set leg next to the truck, and sat down on the hood. I felt relieved. I didn't like sitting around thinking about things like animosity. I got out of the truck and walked over and sat beside him. He pulled out a pack of cigarettes and offered me one.

"No thanks," I said, knowing full well Mama would explode if she smelled tobacco on my breath. She was none too happy about Daddy smoking. She thought it led to worse vices. She posted "No Smoking" signs around the café to discourage him, but he would just go out back, sit on the milk crates, and light up.

Daddy looked wistfully out into the junkyard. "Don't this kind of remind you of the days I used to take you out to watch the Bobcats play baseball? Remember how you used to beg me to let you ride on my shoulders? We'd get home and we'd be carrying on so much your Mama would think I was drunk."

I looked at him in disgust and wondered if he could read the contempt in my eyes. *Yeah, Daddy. Then you got the DWIs and lost your trucker's license. Then Mama got pregnant and sick and the hospital bills piled up. Then you robbed Smitty's liquor store and got thrown in prison.*

And while you were gone, I got too big to ride on your shoulders.

I hopped down from the hood of the truck in irritation. I looked at him and said, "As I recall, you *were* drunk."

I started to walk back around and get in the cab of the truck but Daddy grabbed my shoulder hard and stopped me. With his other hand he thrust the leg of the swing set toward me. At first I thought he was going to hit me with it. Then

I realized he was handing it to me. He gestured out toward the dilapidated Chevy and the broken bottles. "Want to give it a try?"

"Nope."

"Might do you a world of good."

I grabbed the swing set leg out of Daddy's hand, walked over to the old junker, jumped up on the hood, and proceeded to beat the windshield with the metal pole.

Again and again and again. And again.

A large crack started to form in the glass and then another.

After a while I didn't see anything but red and all I could hear was the *whack, crack, whack* of my rhythm. Then all at once the windshield crumbled into pieces and fell into the front seat of the car. That brought me out of my trance. I looked down at my hands. They were shaking. I looked at the Chevy. It looked as if some crazy person had taken after it. That scared me.

I hopped down off the car. Then I walked back to the truck and handed Daddy the leg. He watched me wide-eyed as I resumed my seat on the hood.

"Damn, son. You got a little repressed rage?"

I was breathing so hard I could barely speak. "Not anymore."

Daddy laughed in understanding, breaking the tension between us. I didn't mean to, but I smiled. I guess it was all a little ridiculous.

Then we sat there in silence. I wanted to say something,

but what do you say to someone who's been away in prison for three years?

When I was on the football team, all the other boys had their moms and dads cheering for them in the stands. I didn't have either. I wondered if I should tell him how I felt about not having a daddy all those years, or maybe ask him what it was like not having a family. Or maybe avoid the subject.

I wanted to know what it was like to be mad enough to kill somebody and if he'd ever reached that point.

"Was it tough, being in prison?" was all I could manage to say.

"Prison ain't so bad. If you keep to yourself and do what you're told. You get three square meals and a roof over your head. I been worse places than prison."

I thought about the café and wondered if it was worse than prison. "Is it hard staying sober?" I asked.

Daddy took a long drag off his cigarette. "It's hell, but it's better than being drunk all the time." He looked at the pieces of broken bottle. "I guess."

He didn't sound too sure and that made me nervous. Please be normal, Daddy, I wanted to say.

"You gotta put your life in order to stay sober. To make it work. That's the hard part, setting things straight, making things right. Like taking responsibility. Getting a job. Making amends. One day I'm gonna have to face old Smitty and try to set right what I done to him, pulling that gun on him. That's why I went to his place. To pay him back what I owed him."

Wouldn't it have been easier to send a certified check? But he didn't ask for my advice, so I didn't offer any.

I was troubled by all the lies, but I was also getting used to them, the way a person gets used to being blind.

"I gotta clean up my side of the street. That's all you can do in this life." Daddy tousled my hair and smiled. "C'mon. Let's get back home before your mama whoops both our butts."

———

After that Mama let Daddy do more work around the café, mostly to keep him from looking for another job, I guessed. We worked like crazy all that next week. He and I waxed the floors and he showed me how to use a buffer. Then we did some repairs on the house. Our shack originally belonged to Mama's granddaddy and sat on a farm just outside of town. Then he sold the farm and moved the house into Comfort. When he died he left it to Mama. When Mama bought the café, she had the house hauled on a flatbed trailer and set out back. It wasn't worth moving, to tell the truth. With every relocation the cracks in the walls got bigger. Mama kept a pile of sheet metal out back so I could nail it over the spots where the house separated. We'd stuff the smaller holes with steel wool. That pretty much kept out the mice and larger vermin, but it didn't quite keep out the cold.

Daddy decided all that sheet metal made the house look like a singlewide trailer. He got it in his mind to take it off and plaster the house properly. But that proved to be too much of a project, so we just plastered over the sheet metal. Then we applied some stucco. I felt proud when we were done. It almost looked like a real house, except for the tilt to one side. Daddy wanted to haul the unsightly pile of spare sheet metal off to the dump, but Mama wouldn't let him. She never threw anything away.

Daddy had become stronger physically while in prison. By the time Saturday night came along, I was exhausted, but he was energized. He played three sets on his guitar without taking a break. I forced myself to drink ten sodas so I'd stay awake to meet Cindy.

While Mama and Daddy cleaned the café, I pretended to go to bed in our house out back. I went into my room, stuffed some pillows under my covers so it would look like I was asleep, then put on my best shirt and grabbed my black poetry notebook. I had managed to copy a few poems and stick them inside while things were slow in journalism class.

I walked out the back door and waited in the shadows. It was Saturday night and the prettiest girl in three counties was coming to pick me up. Me. I stared at my scrawny reflection in the shiny metal of the gas pump and surmised that I was in bad need of a haircut.

If Mama caught me I'd be dead.

If Todd caught me I'd be dead and dismembered.

Cindy pulled up at twelve o'clock in her white Thunderbird. I slipped into the seat next to her. She smelled of perfume and Coca-Cola.

"Where we heading?" I asked.

"San Antonio."

I wished we were going to Dallas and not coming back.

San Antonio was nearly an hour southeast, but it didn't matter. I would have followed her to the moon.

chapter 6

We parked in a secluded alley. Cindy took me by the hand and led me into a dark building filled with cigarette smoke. Her hand felt like silk, but it was hard to concentrate on her skin when I kept looking over my shoulder for the law, Mama, and Todd Anderson.

Cindy and I sat down at a little table. As my eyes adjusted to the dim light I saw that the room was much smaller than I expected. There was a boxing ring up near the front. I figured a slam must be some new kind of wrestling.

"I'll have a cup of Chai," Cindy said to a waitress wearing a black miniskirt. "Have whatever you want, kid, I'm buying," Cindy told me.

"Pepsi," I said, expecting them both to laugh at me because I wasn't ordering liquor. But they didn't. Then I wondered why the management didn't throw us out, since we were underage.

I felt out of place. The room was filled with an odd assortment of people. Bikers in leather jackets, college kids in clothes more ragged than mine.

The waitress returned a few minutes later with a soda for me and a steaming mug filled with dark liquid for Cindy.

"That looks like tea," I said to Cindy.

"It is."

"I'm glad you're not drinking," I said.

Cindy threw back her head and laughed. "They don't serve liquor here. This is a coffeehouse. Where did you think I was taking you, kid, to a bar?"

"Well, yeah," I said honestly.

"This is an after-hours place."

"What do you mean?" I asked.

"People come here after the bars close. They don't serve any liquor."

Just then a spotlight shone on the stage and a referee in a black-and-white-striped shirt hopped up into the ring in front of the crowd.

"Welcome one, welcome all to the third annual Java Jim's Grand Slam." His voice was raspy and loud.

I noticed a sign hanging over the counter that read "Java Jim's," and I assumed that must be the name of the coffeehouse. I relaxed a little. I wasn't breaking quite as many rules as I'd thought.

"In corner one we have the magnificent, the stupendous, the almighty wizardress of words, the rose of prose, 'I live to juxtapose,' San Antonio's own Carmelita Cruz." A thin Hispanic woman with flaming red hair wearing a red silk boxer's robe jumped up on the stage, waving her fists in the air. Another woman, the ring girl, wearing a sequined bathing suit, removed the robe from Carmelita and hung it up in the corner. Carmelita wore red boxing shorts and a matching tank top. She waved at the crowd, who cheered loudly. Then she sat down in a chair next to where her robe was hanging.

"In corner two," continued the referee, " 'I'm alarming, I'm charming, I'm big bad and ugly so don't you mug me'—ladies and gentlemen, all the way from Hereford, Texas, the Duke of Diction, Billy Bob Brown."

The audience roared as a huge man in a cowboy hat wearing a blue robe jumped up on the stage, which buckled beneath his weight. The sequined ring girl removed his robe to reveal a huge, flabby gut hanging over a pair of blue shorts. Billy Bob wore steel-toed cowboy boots that showed off his fat, hairy legs.

"My Lord," I gasped. "There's Roy junior in twenty years."

Cindy looked at the cowboy and laughed.

"He's gonna massacre her," I said, thinking the competition was terribly one-sided.

"Just wait and see," smiled Cindy.

Billy Bob took his seat and the referee continued. "Ten rounds, a five-minute maximum per round. The decision of the judges is totally arbitrary and absolutely final. May the best man (or woman) win."

The referee stepped down and Carmelita approached the microphone and spoke. "Don't call me Woman," she yelled.

The women in the crowd hollered and clapped, including Cindy. I couldn't figure out what was going on. I thought she might be trying to intimidate Billy Bob, which didn't seem like a very good idea, considering his size relative to hers. Carmelita continued:

> Don't call me Woman.
> Don't call me Lady.
> Don't call me Love,
> Don't call me Baby.
> Don't call me Honey, Sweetie Pie, Darlin',
> Sugar or Muffin Ball.
> Do me a favor,
> Don't call me at all.

The women in the crowd roared again. One stood up on a table and yelled, "Tell 'em sister." When the roars died down, Carmelita continued:

> I'm not your pet, your child, your kitten.
> I'm not impressed.
> I am not smitten.
> If you say I fight like a girl,
> I will rearrange your world.
> Don't give me flowers.
> Don't give me grief.

Tell me you're leaving.
Give me relief.

She screamed that last line, and then she stood there in silence. A hush fell over the crowd. When she spoke again, Carmelita's voice got very quiet. I thought I saw a tear in her eye or maybe it was just the lights.

> *So why do I cry*
> *When I see you go?*
> *They ask me why?*
> *I just don't know.*
> *It's Goodbye, adios, ciao, adieu.*
> *I needed a friend.*
> *It could have been you.*

Carmelita sat down and the crowd went wild with applause, men and women and me included. Cindy stood up and whistled. I stood up and whistled without even thinking about what I was doing.

But then I felt confused. "I don't get it," I told Cindy when we sat down again. "When are they gonna fight?"

"It's not a real fight. It's a poetry slam."

"Wow" was all I could say.

I felt an electric charge surge through my body. These people were fighting with words. But they weren't really fighting each other. It was as if Carmelita was struggling with some internal demon. I'd never seen someone express so much emotion and keep it so contained at the same time. It was a revelation for me.

Billy Bob Brown walked up to the mike, his gut jiggling like Jell-O with every move he made. He began to recite:

> Two John Deere tractors diverged into a yellow
>   haze.
> One went out to plow the wheat.
> And one went out to plow the maize.
> Being a farm boy, long I stood.
> Thinking I should follow.
> Instead I walked back to the house.
> Watched Oprah, then Geraldo.

He recited another poem about being fat when he was a kid and how he didn't have many friends. It made me feel sorry for telling Roy junior to leave me alone every time he wanted to tag along. Billy Bob went on to tell how he became a rodeo clown and then he had a lot of friends because not only was he funny, he was saving the lives of all the rodeo stars. His poetry was humorous and sad at the same time and I found myself laughing and crying in the same breath. His energy was totally different from that of Carmelita's. It was more drawn inward, while hers was outward.

They took turns reciting poems for ten rounds. By the end I felt exhausted. Then the judges declared Carmelita the winner for the second year in a row. They gave her a trophy of a gold coffee mug and a bouquet of flowers. She gave the flowers to Billy Bob Brown and kissed him on the cheek.

I buzzed all the way home. "I never heard poetry read like that," I told Cindy.

"Now you know why I love it," she said.

"Yeah. I guess I do."

All I could think about was Cindy and me in Johnson City for an entire day, reciting poetry.

"Have you picked your other poems for the district competition?" asked Cindy.

"I'm almost done with my Diversity and the Human Experience category. I got 'Invictus' by Henley, 'Caged Bird' by Maya Angelou, and I'm looking through a book of poems by Naomi Shihab Nye—*Words Under the Words*. There's one called 'Kindness' and another one about saying 'yes' when you really mean 'no.'"

"'Minnows,'" said Cindy. "You know she lives in San Antonio?"

"Yeah."

"How's your other category coming along?"

"Not too good. I got a Shakespeare sonnet and something by Byron."

"Read me the one by Byron," she said with interest, turning on the overhead light so I could see.

"Not that one," I said, trying to hide my panic. I'd chosen it because it reminded me of Cindy.

"Quit stalling." She smiled.

I reluctantly picked my notebook up from the floorboard of the car and slowly opened it to the poem by Byron. I lowered my voice until it was nearly a whisper, hoping not to sound like an idiot. I began:

> *She walks in beauty, like the night*
> *Of cloudless climes and starry skies,*
> *And all that's best of dark and bright*
> *Meet in her aspect and her eyes;*

I wished I could see Cindy's eyes but she kept them fixed on the road in front of her, almost like she was purposely avoiding looking at me. I wondered what those eyes might tell me.

"Go on" was all she said. So I skipped ahead and continued:

> *One shade the more, one ray the less,*
> *Had half impaired the nameless grace*
> *Which waves in every raven tress*
> *Or softly lightens o'er her face,*

Where thoughts serenely sweet express
How pure, how dear their dwelling-place.

I finished the second verse and still she didn't look at me. I was starting to feel like a real sap. It occurred to me that a Texas boy with a drawl as thick as wet cement really shouldn't read the English poets aloud, but I was almost done so I couldn't just stop:

> *And on that cheek and o'er that brow*
> *So soft, so calm, yet eloquent,*
> *The smiles that win, the tints that glow*
> *But tell of days in goodness spent,*
> *A mind at peace with all below,*
> *A heart whose love is innocent!*

I finished the poem and closed my notebook. Cindy never stopped looking at the road. She didn't say anything but she sniffled and wiped a tear from her cheek.

Wow, I got to her.

I just kept looking at her, thinking how much poetry her face could inspire. Mrs. Peterson was right. Words really do have power.

"That was great," she finally said. She still didn't look at me. "But you're not supposed to memorize the poems. I mean, you can memorize them, but it's supposed to look like a reading." She finally glanced at me and I saw sadness in her eyes. She quickly turned her gaze back toward the road.

"Oh" was all I said. I suddenly realized I'd never looked at the notebook. I'd stared at her the whole time. I didn't even realize I'd memorized the poem. Even so, I didn't think she would get troubled over that. There was something more. Something she wasn't saying. What I wanted to ask was *What are the words under your words, Cindy?*

We didn't say anything the rest of the way home. I just sat there in silence trying to read her mind.

I wish I'd never asked you to the slam, Kenny?

I like you, but dating a freshman would destroy my social life?

What am I doing out on a Saturday night with a scrawny kid with holes in his jeans?

When Cindy pulled up in front of the café it was nearly four o'clock in the morning. In two hours Mama would be expecting me to open up the café. I wanted to hurry inside my house as quickly as possible to avoid any further awkwardness. I grabbed the door handle, ready to open it and sprint toward home.

Cindy turned off the engine. She turned toward me and smiled. "You know, Kenny, you're the only person I could ever consider taking to Java Jim's."

"Yeah?" I said, loosening my grip on the door.

She leaned close to me and her lips were just inches from mine.

I stopped breathing.

"You're gonna be so great in Johnson City," she said, leaning closer.

But the spell was broken by a *thud* against the glass. I looked up to see Mama pounding on my window. Rage blazed in her eyes. Every good feeling I'd felt that night was suddenly replaced with dread.

chapter 7

"*Give me one good reason why* I shouldn't ground you for the rest of your life?" Mama hollered so loud, she could have awoken the dead in Fredericksburg, Boerne, and Welfare.

Cindy and I stood up against the car like two thugs waiting to be frisked. I saw Roy junior peeking out from behind the curtains of the house. If Daddy was awake, he didn't make an appearance.

"Please don't tell my daddy about this, Mrs. Willson," pleaded Cindy.

"Hush up," said Mama. "I'll deal with you next."

From where I was standing, the UIL competition and Johnson City looked as if it was on another planet. I had to think fast. "We were checking something out for the café."

Mama's eyes narrowed suspiciously, but they also softened a tiny bit. "Keep talking," she said.

"We went to an after-hours club," I said.

"It's a place where people go after the bars close," said Cindy, following my lead. "They don't serve any liquor."

"So we went to check it out 'cause we thought maybe the café could become an after-hours club."

I could tell that Mama's brain was chewing on the idea. "Go on."

"People coming home from partying in San Antonio or Fredericksburg might stop at the café if they saw it was open," said Cindy.

"And truckers might be glad to find a place by the highway opened all night," I added.

Mama rubbed her chin in thought.

Daddy finally emerged from the house. He wore a pair of blue jeans, no shirt, no shoes, and he carried Roy junior.

"Kenny busted," said Roy junior.

"What's going on?" asked Daddy.

"Nothing," said Mama. The snarl on her face had slowly turned into a smile. "Get in the house," she told me.

She didn't say another word about me going to San Antonio. Daddy never mentioned it at all.

The next day she told me to make a new sign for the café. It read "Gas, Food, Expresso Bar, Live Music. Open All Night."

"Are you gonna tell your mama she misspelled espresso?" Jake asked.

"I don't *tell* Mama nothing," I replied.

I didn't realize working at the café could get worse, but that's exactly what happened once we started staying open twenty-four hours a day. I got home from school, worked until midnight, later on the weekends. Sometimes all night.

On school days I'd sleep until five o'clock in the morning, then I'd get up and get dressed and take over for Mama until I went to my first-period class. I'd wake her up just before I left so she could get as much sleep as possible. If the new schedule was hard on me, it must have been murder on her because as far as I could tell, the only time she slept was between 5:00 A.M. and 7:00 A.M. She wouldn't let Daddy help during the day because she said he needed his rest so he'd be fit to perform on his guitar. He got fuming mad and started talking about putting in an application at the hardware store where at least he could "work like a man." So Mama finally let him run the café in the afternoons so she could take a nap.

I nearly got detention when I fell asleep in computer class four days in a row. But I didn't complain about the long hours at the café to Mama. For one thing, the idea of an after-hours spot took off. We actually started getting customers in the early morning, just like Cindy and I had predicted. Mama was happy for the first time in years.

Second, the UIL competition in Johnson City was in a few days, during the St. Patrick's day weekend, and I didn't want to do anything to rock the boat. Ever since the slam, I'd been practicing my poems every spare minute.

I took the book of poetry Cindy had given me and hid it under the bathroom sink. After I cleaned out the pile of Hershey's wrappers, that is. It was the same place Daddy used to hide his liquor. It was the one place Mama wouldn't find the book, because she had a bad habit of never looking for things she didn't want to see. Even though the house was cluttered with junk, Mama never put anything under the bathroom sink. It was as if she suspected Daddy might start hiding liquor again and she didn't want to know about it if he did.

Friday night I cleaned out the fryer and then tried to read. Roy junior, wearing a diaper and a cowboy hat, got up on stage between sets and shook a box of uncooked macaroni, singing, "Shake, shake, shake. Shake your booty." He got no one's attention so he hollered, "Hey look, me a singing cowboy."

"That's nice," I said, looking up from the biography I was researching on Henley. I returned to my book. I was hoping to find something inspiring for my introduction.

Roy junior dropped his box of macaroni and crawled up on my lap. "Read me a story, Kenny," he said.

So I read out loud from my book. "Robert Louis Stevenson and Henley became friends after Stevenson visited him in the Edinburgh infirmary. In fact, Stevenson's Long John Silver character was inspired by Henley."

"Long John Silver's fish and more?" asked Roy junior.

"No, silly, the one-legged pirate from *Treasure Island*." I tousled his hair.

About three in the morning a group of folks stopped in

on their way home from partying in San Antonio. They clapped to the rhythm of Daddy's music. Mama even danced between the tables while she took their food orders. Part of me knew I needed to say something to her. I couldn't just leave for Johnson City the next morning without reminding her I was going. But another part of me was afraid to say anything that might distress her. Every time I thought about speaking up, I felt a huge knot in my stomach. Daddy took a break, sat down on one of the barstools, and drank a soda.

"Kenny," said Mama. "In the morning I'm gonna need you to go over to Food Warehouse in Boerne and pick up some more coffee filters. We're almost out."

"But Mama, remember, I'm going to the UIL meet in Johnson City." I felt as if I'd swallowed my daddy's guitar.

"The UI—what?"

"Remember, Mama, it's a competition for newswriting and stuff like that."

"Dang, I forgot all about that, Kenny. Well, don't worry. I'll write you an excuse. Anyway, it ain't right, them making you do extra schoolwork on the weekends."

I saw Daddy studying my reaction, which must have been close to panic, over the top of his soda straw. Mama didn't seem to notice at all. She had the power to destroy my dreams with a word. What gave her the right to do that?

I followed Mama back and forth between the coffeemaker and the sink. "They're not *making* me go. It's something I elected to do."

"I'm sure it all sounds like a lot of fun." Mama whacked the side of the machine as black coffee sputtered out. "They try to make it sound fun. Then you get down there and it's a bunch of waiting around and when you finally get to do something, it's just like being at school."

I didn't know where to begin to argue with her logic. Mama had never competed in anything at school. She hadn't even finished school. She'd dropped out in the tenth grade. She didn't know what going to Johnson City would be like. "But they're counting on me" was all I could think to say.

"So am I," said Mama, putting her hands on her hips. Daddy walked up behind her and spun her around. He kissed her and got her all giggly again.

"Maggie, did I ever show you how we made coffee in prison?" Daddy set the full pot on the extra burner and started a new one. He ripped a paper towel from the roll hanging above the sink. Then he put it in the coffeemaker in the place where the filter was supposed to go. Then he scooped in the coffee grounds and poured in the water. "They don't got much over there in Hondo, but they do know how to make a dang good pot of coffee."

Mama watched as black coffee filled the pot. "That's a handy trick," she said.

"I guess we could go a day or two without filters," Daddy replied, taking another sip of soda.

I saw what he was trying to do and I could have hugged him. In that moment, I loved him.

"That ain't the point," said Mama. "The café's just now getting going."

Mama, I hated.

Daddy nuzzled Mama's ear with his nose and whispered, "Don't you think we need a day without a chaperone?"

Mama turned three shades of red and I got to go to Johnson City.

———

The competition proved to be anything but boring. Early that morning, all of us in the poetry-interpretation segment crowded into a classroom and waited anxiously while one of the judges pulled a letter out of a hat.

"A," said the judge. "Diversity and the Human Experience." That meant that everyone had to read performance A for the preliminary competition. Half the room let out a groan, the other half a sigh of relief. I was one of the happy ones. I felt way more prepared for that category than the other one.

Of course, everyone who made it to the final round would still have to read from category B, Words of Inspiration.

They broke us up into two groups and we all squeezed into two different classrooms for the preliminary rounds. Francesca Adams wasn't signed up for that event, but she and her parents came to watch. Francesca ran track in addition to being a spelling champion.

I was one of the first ones up. I was glad I didn't have

to sit around stewing, thinking about how good everyone else was.

I gave my introduction, then started with Maya Angelou. When I read about how the "caged bird sings of freedom," I couldn't help but think of my daddy strumming his guitar in a prison cell. I wondered if he felt free now that he was out, or if he still felt caged.

Next I read "Minnows," by Naomi Shihab Nye. I finished with Henley's "Invictus." By the time I sat down, I was buzzing. I knew I'd done good.

But after about twenty minutes of listening to other students read, that feeling passed. Everybody was good. Cindy was the best, but there was also this boy from Blanco who had everybody in tears by the time he was done. I felt my chances of making it to the final round lessen as each minute ticked away.

I hated to leave Cindy to go to the newswriting competition. A group of about twenty of us sat at desks in a room with yellow walls. The moderator, a woman with brown, beehive-styled hair, handed us all a sheet of paper containing a list of boring facts related to an automobile accident. We had one hour to rewrite the boring details into an interesting news story. The sportswriting contest was more of the same, except the car wreck was replaced by the quarterback of a fictitious high school breaking his leg during the fourth quarter of the homecoming game.

As soon as I came out of the newswriting competition I heard a voice come over the intercom: "Results from the preliminary rounds of the poetry-interpretation competition will be announced in the cafeteria in five minutes."

I hurried inside the cafeteria and found Cindy. She grabbed my hand and held it tight as we waited expectantly. I don't think she meant much by the gesture, but I felt fire spread from my fingers all through my body.

One of the judges read the top three names from the other round. Then he got to ours—"Cindy Blackwell, Tina Hoffman, Kenny Willson."

Cindy shrieked and hugged my neck. "We made it, kid."

Across the room I saw the boy from Blanco stuff his poetry notebook in a trash can in frustration.

After that there was some sitting around and waiting, as Mama had predicted. But what Mama couldn't know was how quickly those hours of waiting passed in the company of Cindy Blackwell. She and Francesca Adams taught me how to play chess on a little magnetic board Cindy had brought in her purse. Then they made me practice reciting my poems about a dozen times each.

"That kid from Blanco was really good. Why didn't he make it to the final round?" I asked Cindy.

"Did you see the way he turned two pages at once, then turned back one page so he'd be in the right place?"

"Yeah, so?"

"They count off for that," said Francesca.

"Really? Why?"

Cindy reached across the chessboard and took my queen with her rook. "Your performance has to be flawless. The competition's too stiff."

I got nervous all of a sudden. "So what should he have done?"

"He should have kept going without looking back. He should have recited it from memory," said Cindy.

"But you said not to do that."

"It's not supposed to *look* like you memorized it."

My head was spinning. *Memorize it, but pretend that you didn't.* I made a mental note not to turn too many pages at once.

I was just getting out of the sportswriting competition when I ran into Cindy, who was finishing the editorial writing contest.

She grabbed me by the arm. "Hurry or we're gonna be late."

We ran all the way to the room where the poetry reading was scheduled.

I felt a little weird about competing against Cindy, but I figured she'd beat me and it would be okay. I thought about Carmelita and Billy Bob and felt my confidence growing.

When we got to the room it was already my turn to go up. I hadn't even had a chance to sit down. I walked up to the podium and stood up in front of the judges, ready to take on the world.

I gave my introduction and that went okay, but when I started to read the poem, something strange happened as soon as I opened my mouth:

> *Two roads diverged in a yellow wood,*
> *And sorry I could not travel both*

At first the words stuck to the roof of my mouth like peanut butter on white bread. Then it got worse. I could actually hear and feel my voice shaking. I didn't understand why my voice was trembling. I wasn't nervous. Or at least I didn't think I was. I must have been winded from running:

> *And be one traveler, long I stood.*

It got worse.

This should not be happening. I am not nervous. I need to catch my breath, that's all.

I looked at the judges, expecting one of them to throw me out. They just smiled back at me. Couldn't they see I was falling apart? I looked at Cindy. She winked. That made me even more nervous.

> *And looked down one as far as I could*

The shaking got worse. Why couldn't I control my own vocal cords, I wondered? A glass of water sat on the podium. I stopped and sipped it.

To where it bent in the undergrowth;

It didn't help. By that time I was very anxious. I wanted to hide under the podium. There was a minor earthquake occurring in my throat.

Then took the other, as just as fair,

I'd heard of panic attacks. I'd thought they were a bunch of nonsense until now. My heart beat so fast I felt I was going into cardiac arrest. My palms turned sweaty and my breathing got so shallow that I had to stop to inhale after every two words:

And having . . . perhaps . . . the better . . . claim.
Because . . . it was . . . grassy . . . and wanted . . .
wear . . .

A little voice in my head said, "You're gonna die, run . . . Run . . . RUN . . ."

I grabbed ahold of the podium to keep my feet from taking off without the rest of me. I hurried through the poem.

Then I sprinted through the others. Then I closed my note-book and rushed into the hall. I was hyperventilating.

Cindy followed me out.

"How bad was it?" I asked.

"What are you talking about? You were great. I loved the way you paused after each line, like you really were at a crossroads, trying to sort out your path."

I had one thought on my mind. *I will never do that again as long as I live.*

I won first place for newswriting and sportswriting and Cindy won first place for editorial writing. I was so excited, I forgot about my flopped performance with the poetry un-til I heard the results of that competition. Cindy won first place, which I'd expected.

"And you won third," she said.

I hadn't even gone to the cafeteria when they announced the poetry category over the intercom, because I knew I'd done so badly.

"Don't kid me like that," I said.

"No, really, you won third. I guess they liked your inter-pretation."

I ran over to the paper hanging next to the door of the room where I'd read (or rather assaulted) my poems. There it was. *Third Place—Willson, Kenny.*

I looked again. I had definitely won third. I had to find some way to get out of doing another poetry reading at the next stage of the competition. There were no two ways about it. I thought about protesting my own placing, but I didn't think that would go over too well with the judges.

Cindy and I sat together in the back of the bus with our medals and the sheets with the judges' comments between us. The bus was filled with excited conversation. Mrs. Peterson always had a lot of winners from Comfort High. Those who hadn't won just sounded relieved to be done.

"In five weeks we'll go to Southwest Texas State University in San Marcos," said Cindy. That's where the regional competition would be held.

Five weeks. I had a little over a month to figure out how to disqualify myself from the poetry reading without getting bumped from my other two events.

"I can check out the school while I'm there. I applied for the fall but I haven't heard from them yet. They have a great English department. I'm going to be an English teacher."

"You'll be good at it," I said. Twilight fell and the little lights along the aisle of the bus came on. It had been a long day. I felt exhausted and excited all at the same time. Everybody started to quiet down.

Cindy closed her eyes as if in a dream. "I'll have every summer off and I'm going to travel. I want to visit all the cafés in Paris where Hemingway used to hang out. If I don't get accepted at San Marcos, maybe I'll get into Texas Women's University in Denton. Those were my top two choices."

"Denton," I said with interest, momentarily forgetting my recent near-death experience. "Isn't Denton near Dallas, Cindy?"

"A few miles away," she said. "Why are you smiling?"

"Nothing," I said. But I was thinking how I'd just fit the name "Cindy" and the word "Dallas" into the same sentence.

"Todd is going to Texas A&M. He's gonna study agriculture. Todd isn't so bad. He'll probably finish school and come home to help his father on the sheep farm. They're a nice family. Todd's okay when we're alone, but when he gets around the guys he's a little rough around the edges."

"Rough?" I said. "I think the appropriate term is 'serrated.'"

Cindy laughed, then she got real quiet. "He asked me to go to the prom."

"What? You're not going, are you?" My dream suddenly started to unravel.

"It's just the prom and the graduation parties. Too bad you aren't a senior, kid." She tousled my hair playfully.

"Would it make a difference?" I asked solemnly.

The playful look left her face and she looked out the window, avoiding my eyes again. "Yeah, it makes a difference."

The words under the words. She liked me but she wished she didn't. I couldn't blame her. Who was I? Some short kid three years younger than she was.

We rode home the rest of the way in silence, giving me plenty of time to stew about poetry and Todd Anderson. I wanted to tell her that she could do better than Todd, but I kept my mouth shut.

Monday morning the word around school was that Cindy and Todd were back together. I saw her at lunch. She was sitting with Todd and wearing his jacket, which must have been uncomfortable in that humidity. She smiled and laughed at his stupid jokes.

How can you be attracted to a Neanderthal like Todd Anderson?

And if she wasn't attracted to him, if she was just going with him to the end-of-the-year parties, was that better or worse?

I stuffed my medals under the bathroom sink next to the book of poems.

Then I counted my Dallas money. I had just over five hundred dollars. If I won first or even second place at state for either newswriting or sportswriting, I'd have the thousand I needed. I hid the box of cash back under my bed.

Maybe when I got to Dallas I'd forget all about Cindy Blackwell.

No.

Maybe when Cindy went to Denton she'd forget about Todd Anderson.

Whatever happened, I would definitely forget about poetry.

chapter 8

The café not only took off as an after-hours spot, but kids from school started hanging out there on Friday nights after the basketball game. Most of them had to pass the café on the way home and there was nowhere else to go, so they came to Roy's Place.

On the Friday after the district competition, Cindy told me at lunch that she and Todd would stop by after the game.

A little voice in my head said *Beware*.

I told the voice to shut up.

I got out the iron and pressed my best pair of jeans and a button-down shirt Jake gave me for Christmas. Then I dug my St. Christopher medal out of the dishwater I was cleaning it in and put it back on the piece of leather it hung on. I never took it off except to clean it. The silver medallion depicting the patron saint of travelers was my prize possession. It used to belong to Grandpa Harris. The piece of leather was from his army boot from when he was in boot camp. He never actually made it to the army. He got kicked out for being a conscientious objector, he'd told me, but I never found out what he'd objected to. Grandpa Harris had given me the medal and the bootlace when he visited Comfort. "I'm heading to Dallas to try my hand at worm farming. Look me up if you ever get north, kid," he'd said.

"What's got into you?" Mama asked me as she looked me up and down.

"I just want to look nice for Daddy's performance tonight," I lied.

I'd dropped a hint to Mama that she should let Daddy go to the basketball game, to help him relax before singing all night. And, of course, he needed someone to drive him. It wasn't difficult to convince her. Mama always worried that Daddy needed to relax.

"When he gets worked up he does crazy things," she'd told me more than once.

She beamed with pride, thinking I'd gotten dressed up for Daddy. "I like to see the way you two have been hanging out together."

"It ain't exactly 'hanging out,' Mama. We've just been fixing up the café and the house."

"All the same. I know it means a lot to your daddy. Sometimes he feels like you've had to take on too much of his responsibility. He thinks you might be angry, even though I try to tell you you ain't. I can't seem to make him understand how much we are all pulling for him."

"I gotta go, Mama. I gotta drive Daddy." I didn't feel angry until she started talking about how I wasn't. Suddenly I was pissed off again.

She gave me a big hug. It caught me off guard because

she hadn't done that for a while. She squeezed me so hard I thought she'd push all the air out of me. But she felt warm and good and I felt myself hugging her back. Then she pulled back and there were tears in her eyes. She tried to wipe them away before I saw.

"I'm the one you oughta be upset with. Working you as hard as I do."

I didn't say anything.

"It just takes so much to keep this café going and I can't do it all alone. I need you, honey. I wish I didn't, but I do."

"I know," I said, choking on the words. I realized then how tired Mama looked. More than tired, she looked weary of living. With the café staying open all night, she wasn't getting enough sleep. Even with Daddy helping out. Sure she worked me hard, but only half as hard as she worked herself. I suddenly felt guilty for planning to run off to Dallas.

I worried about who would pick up the slack when I left. What if the café fell apart without me? What would happen to her then? What would happen to Roy junior? He barely had a mama as it was.

I wondered if Daddy felt guilty when he looked into Mama's tired eyes. Maybe he had good reason to feel that way.

Were things really that bad for me? I asked myself. After all, I still had school and journalism. I was still popular, even if I didn't do band or football anymore. I wasn't going to be anybody in a big town like Dallas. At least I was somebody in Comfort.

Mama looked beautiful to me just then. I saw something in her that I recognized in myself. The unwavering desire to do something with her life and the unwillingness to let anything stand in her way.

Mama reached into her pocket and handed me a ten-dollar bill. "Here, take this. Buy yourself a hot dog or something. You and Daddy have a good time."

I took the crumpled money. It looked as tired and worn out as she did. I hugged her neck. "I love you, Mama," I blurted out before thinking about being too old to say things like that.

"I love you too, honey. I know it's gotta be a lot for you, Kenny. Working in the café and trying to go to school too. Pretty soon it won't be so hard on you."

She sighed and smiled a honey-glazed grin and I wondered what scheme her mind was working on at the moment.

"How come?" I asked.

"Next year you'll be sixteen. Then you can quit."

"Quit what?" I asked nervously. She'd already made me quit nearly everything that meant anything to me and I was pretty sure she didn't mean quit working.

"Quit school."

"Quit school? You want me to quit school?" Was she serious? I felt confused and angry at the same time.

"What are you so riled about?" asked Mama, taking a step back and looking me over as if I was crazy. "Me and your daddy both quit school at sixteen. We didn't miss anything. I thought you'd be happy."

"Happy! I'm somebody at school. I ain't nobody here at the café." I was so angry, my voice shook.

"You're ungrateful. That's what you are, Kenny Willson."

I clenched my fists and felt the corners of the ten-dollar bill scraping my hand. Mama was the only person who could make me go from love to rage in a matter of seconds. I hated the way she made me feel and I hated myself for letting her jerk around my emotions like she always did.

Sure, I understood dreams, but I would never ask somebody to trade theirs for mine.

"I gotta go." I ran out the door, making a promise to myself to never again feel guilty about leaving Mama.

I was getting out from under her thumb before she used it to squash me beyond repair.

Daddy and I wouldn't be able to stay for all four quarters of the game, but I didn't care. I just wanted to get a look at Cindy before she came over to the café later that night. There were times when she looked so beautiful that I thought I'd swallow my tongue. If Todd saw me gaping at her he'd beat in my head. If I went to the game and kind of worked her out of my system, without anybody looking, maybe I could preserve my skull.

"Want some curly fries to go with that corn dog?" Daddy asked me while people were settling into their seats. He was unusually happy, almost exuberant.

"No thanks," I said. We'd gotten there early and he'd already been to the concession stand three times. I figured he was going out to sneak a smoke.

He went off to get some fries while I scanned the faces in the gym for Cindy and Todd. The teams warmed up and the sound of all those basketballs thumping against the wooden floor echoed like thunder.

I looked at the bobcat and the buck, the school mascots, painted on a map of the state of Texas on the wall across the gym. I got a sick feeling in the pit of my stomach. I thought about the graduation ceremonies held every year in the Bobcat Stadium. The seniors tossed their caps into the air and let out wildcat screams.

I was never going to be one of them. I felt my hatred for Mama welling up inside of me again. I tried to push it down.

Sure, I'd been planning on leaving for Dallas, but I always had it in the back of my mind that if things worked out at home, I could stay and graduate.

Things were never going to work out at home. I knew that for a fact now. I would never graduate and if I stayed I'd be Mama's slave for the rest of my life. If I was old enough to quit school and work for Mama, then I was old enough to go out on my own and work for myself or Grandpa Harris.

He had seemed pretty sure that worms represented the future of agriculture.

My heart skipped a beat when I saw Cindy moving through the bleachers several rows below me. Todd had his arm around her waist. He let his hand brush over her butt as she sat down. She slapped his wrist. "Serves you right," I muttered at Todd under my breath.

"Serves who right?" said a voice next to me. I looked over to see Suzie Blackwell, Cindy's kid sister, sitting down next to me. She snapped a couple of photos of the teams warming up, then she waved at the people who passed by. "Hi, Francesca. Hi, Carrie."

"Hey, Kenny, how's it going?" asked Dr. Adams, Francesca's father.

"Fine, sir. Thanks for asking."

"You gonna play football next year?" he asked.

"It doesn't look likely."

"That's too bad. I enjoyed watching you run."

Dr. Adams always looked relaxed, which I thought was unusual because I figured doctors were overworked. He was a pediatrician in Fredericksburg. His wife, the first black Miss Texas, was an accountant in San Antonio. Most of the people in Comfort like the Adamses were white-collar professionals who commuted to jobs in nearby towns or even San Antonio. They lived in Comfort because they wanted a quiet place to raise their children. I don't know how Mama and Daddy fit into that mix. Perhaps towns, like families, have their black sheep.

"Hi, Mary Jane. Hi Cathy." Suzie just couldn't sit still. I wanted to put my hand on her head to keep her from moving around so much. It made me nervous.

"What does she see in him?" I said, watching Todd plant another obnoxious kiss on Cindy's face.

"He reminds her of our father." Suzie pointed to Buddy Blackwell, a short, stocky ex-marine who stood on a bench screaming, "Kick some butt, Bobcats!"

All of a sudden Suzie got real still and quiet. Then she leaned into me so that our shoulders were touching. It made me more nervous than the wiggling had, especially when she batted her long eyelashes and rolled back her brown eyes and looked up at me as if she was a little baby dachshund.

"Do you have a date for the Sadie Hawkins Dance?"

"The what?" I asked, moving away from her.

"The dance where the girls get to ask out the guys."

I jumped out of my seat, dropping my corn dog. Before she could say another word I said, "I gotta go."

Suzie looked up at me in surprise as the corn dog fell off my plate, hit her lap, rolled off, and landed on the floor. I was too jumpy. Even Cindy's kid sister was making me nervous.

"Go where?" said Daddy, coming up behind me.

"We gotta get back to the café so you can practice."

"But we just got here."

"We gotta *go*, Daddy."

He must have seen the terror in my face because all he said was "Okay," with an understanding smile. As I followed him out to the pickup I noticed for the first time that he stunk to high heaven of cologne. It hadn't bothered me before. I guess my mind had been on other things.

He'd gotten all fixed up for a night out and I'd spoiled it.

Back at the café he tuned his guitar while I wiped down the tables.

"I don't see what you're so upset about. She's a pretty girl."

"She's skinny and she's ugly and she wore braces for nearly four years."

"She ain't wearing braces now and if you ask me, she's got a darn pretty smile."

"She's not my type."

Daddy laughed. "I remember when I was your age. The girls sure did make me nervous. I never knew if I was right-side up or upside down when I was with a girl."

"What about Mama?"

He laughed again. "With your mama I was upside down all the time, but at least I knew what direction I was pointing."

That's exactly how I felt about Cindy and no kid sister with a nice smile or otherwise was going to make me feel right-side up.

Daddy started playing at eight o'clock to a couple of truckers who stopped by for dinner.

Mama walked in carrying Roy junior on her hip. He was

wearing his Batman pajamas and his cowboy boots. Since our house was out back, she wasn't typically in a hurry to dress him. Some days, like today, she never dressed him. If he had on his boots I guess she figured that was good enough. She just let him run around in his boots and pajamas until he peeled them off. Then he ran around in his diaper and boots. Then, around ten at night, she would put him back in his pajamas, take off his boots, and tuck him in a playpen in the back of the café and that's where he would sleep, curled up next to his truck.

The game wouldn't be over until nearly ten, but I found myself looking up at the clock every five minutes anyway. At nine-thirty I broke out in a sweat.

Todd was going to see right through me.

Those truckers left and three more came in. I recognized one as a fairly regular customer Mama called Harold. Jake came in a little while later and perched himself at the counter. It was ten o'clock. I could feel my heart beating inside my throat. Cindy would arrive at any minute.

Mama punched a hole in a coupon card and handed it to Harold. "You get a free pizza with your next fill-up, Harold. Now don't let me hear that you been going over to the Exxon."

"No ma'am, Maggie," said the beer-bellied trucker. "They don't give away pizza down at the Exxon. Say, how's your meat loaf tonight? I have a hankering to try something besides the Frito pie."

"Juiciest meat loaf in three counties, but we just ran out."

"How about the chicken-fried steak?"

"Hand breaded. Served with a pile of creamy mashed potatoes. But we're all out of that too. Not much selection after the dinner rush."

"Dinner rush?" I said. Sure, we were starting to get a steady stream of customers after about ten, but we'd never had any kind of rush. Mama shot me a dirty look, but my mind was on the clock. It was 10:15. Maybe the game had gone into overtime.

Harold closed his menu and handed it to Mama. "Maybe you should just tell me what you do have."

"Today's special is Frito pie. We also have pizza, chili, and heavenly hash."

"Give me a bowl of chili."

I watched the second hand make its way around the clock, then I watched the minute hand click to 10:17. I tried to calculate how long it would take for everybody to get in their cars and leave the school gym. Sometimes traffic got pretty bottlenecked but it couldn't take more than twenty minutes for the whole place to clear. Maybe somebody parked behind Todd's pickup and he couldn't get out.

Then I saw the trail of headlights heading down the highway out front. Any one of them could be Cindy.

Mama went behind the counter and spooned out a bowl of chili.

"Chicken-fried steak, my eye," said Jake.

"Hush up," said Mama.

He smiled and lowered his voice. "You haven't ever had chicken-fried steak. You haven't ever had meat loaf, for that matter. What kind of place are you running here, Maggie? It isn't a restaurant, because you don't cook. And there sure isn't any service to speak of. You got live music, but it isn't a bar, 'cause there isn't any liquor. You don't even allow smoking."

"Roy can't go off singing in bars. You know that."

"Is that why you spent two years working three jobs? So Roy could have a place to sing?"

Mama sprinkled some grated cheese on top of the chili. "I got dreams, Jake. I ain't gonna be a hash queen all my life." She walked off with the chili.

It was 10:20. About ten kids from the basketball game came in and ordered pizza. Cindy and Todd weren't among them.

I watched the clock change to 10:30 and the trail of headlights disappeared. Then it was 10:40 . . . 10:45 . . . 11:00 . . . Cindy wasn't coming.

chapter 9

The rest of the night dragged on like cold molasses. Daddy took a break between sets. As soon as he slipped out the back door, Mama turned on the tape of him singing, so that nobody would miss him while he was having a smoke.

It took me a long time to figure out why Mama wanted to buy that stupid little gas station restaurant. It sat at a crossroads, at the junction of Highway 87 to Fredericksburg and Interstate 10 to San Antonio. Semis raced by all hours of the night just fifty feet from where we slept in our house behind the gas station. When things got slow I would watch the semis go by trailing a spray of rainwater behind them. The roads seemed to lead everywhere. My life led nowhere.

When Daddy got out of prison, Mama's interest in the café got real obvious. Mama became a one-woman promotional company for the talents of Roy Dan Willson, and the café was the showcase for his music. It was a protected environment where no smoking or drinking was allowed and where Mama could watch Daddy like a hawk hovering over a snake as it slithers through the grass.

At first I had thought she bought the café just to get out of her job at Shooters, a club over in San Antonio. She'd told me she was a "professional dancer," but I knew better, even at twelve. She'd go off every night, dumping me with Roy junior and his poop-filled diapers and his colic. I didn't know how to handle a one-year-old, but I learned pretty quick that if I left him in his crib long enough, eventually he'd get tired of screaming his head off and go to sleep. I'd lay in bed listening to him holler, sometimes until midnight, plugging my ears with cotton balls and cursing my daddy for conveniently getting himself thrown in jail, where I was sure he was snoring away as peacefully as a hibernating bear.

Every morning, when I woke up, Mama would just be getting home, her face still painted up like a geisha girl. She'd always make us a hot breakfast. I knew she felt guilty about something because that was the only period in her life when she actually cooked for us. That's why it was such a shock to me when, one year later, she told me she'd saved enough money from working at Shooters to buy a café.

"What do you want with a café? You hate to cook," I told her. She threw a shoe at me. But as it ended up, she didn't actually cook at the café. She mostly served frozen pizzas, other microwavables, and honey buns.

A man in a cowboy hat walked in and handed Mama a credit card. She admired his blue eighteen-wheeler out the window as she waited for the card to clear. "That's quite a rig, Keith."

"Just paid her off," said the man.

I waited for the coffee to brew. Mama always gave away a

free cup of coffee with each fill-up. The coffeemaker, which Mama had purchased at a going-out-of-business sale from the Hoot Owl Café, was hissing and spitting more than usual. I whacked it on the side and thick black liquid sputtered out. There were grounds in it, but the truckers never seemed to mind. It was 12:30 and we hadn't had any other customers for over half an hour. I hoped Mama would close the place for at least a few hours, but I knew she'd never dream of it. She lived in constant fear that she might miss the once-in-a-lifetime opportunity to make Daddy famous.

"You ever get up north, toward Nashville?" asked Mama, handing the man back his credit card.

"From time to time."

A charming smile broke across Mama's face. Her mind was chewing on an idea and it scared me. "I do respect you truck drivers. It's a hard life out on the road." She looked over at me. "Hurry up with that coffee, Kenny. Keith has a deadline."

I gave the machine another whack.

She seemed to be flirting with him, but I knew better. Keith turned red in the face. "My husband used to drive a rig." Mama batted her eyelashes at the man and smiled like a teenager.

"That so?" said Keith.

"But he don't do it anymore. He's a singer now. That's him over the speakers."

Keith squinted and listened closely to the country-and-western music. "Dang, I thought that was Randy Travis."

Mama threw back her head and let out a laugh. The first sincere thing I'd seen her do in the last ten minutes. "Heck no! That ain't Randy Travis. That's my Roy. He wrote that song for the café. Lyrics and all."

I handed Keith a cup of coffee in a Styrofoam cup.

"Your husband has quite a talent." He turned to leave. "Thanks for the coffee, ma'am."

"Wait!" yelled Mama. "You get a free sandwich with that fill-up too."

"I do?" said Keith, walking back to the counter.

"He does?" I said. I wondered how long she could keep the café afloat with all the stuff she gave away.

"Kenny, fix this nice man a roast beef sandwich." Then she dropped her voice so that only I could hear. "And don't use that old meat. Get out the fresh stuff I bought at the butcher's yesterday."

I reluctantly went to the back to get the meat out of the refrigerator and noticed that the back door was standing ajar. I started to close it, but then I thought I could use a little fresh air. I stepped outside. Daddy was having a smoke, drinking coffee out of a thermos and staring at the stars. The coffee must have been old because it wasn't steaming as it usually did on cool nights. At least the nights were still cool even though the days were warming up. When summer hit, it would be sweltering hot even after dark.

"You want me to get you some hot coffee?" I asked Daddy. "I just brewed a fresh pot."

Daddy jumped up and knocked over his thermos, spilling the contents. "Kenny, you liked to scared me to death. Don't be sneaking up on your old man that way." He picked up the thermos and quickly screwed the lid on, then he sat back down. I remembered how he used to hide liquor in his coffee thermos, but I shook the idea away telling myself that I hadn't seen Daddy acting drunk.

"You want some more coffee?" I asked again.

"Nah, I need to be heading back in. Sit down here for a minute."

I pulled up another milk crate and sat beside him. He pointed up at the sky. "You see that big star? That's Polaris."

I looked up. I couldn't tell one from another. "They all look the same to me."

"It's in the handle of the Little Dipper."

I looked again. This time I made it out. "I see it."

"That's the North Star. It's always in the same place and that place is always due north. All the other ones move around, but that one stays the same. If you ever get lost and lose your bearings, remember that."

"I will," I said, but I thought that a map would serve me better.

"When you're in the big city you don't get views of the sky like this. Personally, I prefer the way things look from out here in the country."

Mama stuck her head outside. "Kenny, that man is waiting on his sandwich. Get a move on." She hurried back inside as I stood up.

"But I think your Mama has other ideas," said Daddy.

I wasn't sure if he was talking about the stars or the city or the sandwiches.

I started to go inside, but Daddy put a hand on mine to stop me. "I ain't been much of a daddy to you these last few years. I know you been taking on a lot of the load around here."

I squirmed away from him. "It's nothing." It was one thing to go goo-goo-eyed over Mama. I sure wasn't going to do that with Daddy.

"I'm gonna make it up to you, son. I'm gonna get a real job and I'm gonna set things straight around here. I'll show you what I'm really made of . . . you and your mama." He said that last part almost as if he meant in spite of Mama. "I'm gonna have another smoke. Tell Maggie I'll be in shortly."

"I will." I went inside, grabbed the meat, threw together a sandwich, wrapped it in paper and took it out front. My heart nearly stopped when I saw Cindy sitting in a booth next to Todd Anderson. He kept putting his arm around her shoulder and leaning on her as if he was a bombardier jacket and she was a coat rack. She pushed him off in disgust. Petey and R.J. and their dates squeezed into the booth with them.

The boys looked as if they'd been drinking.

Cindy looked as if she'd been crying.

I handed the sandwich to Mama. She put it inside a box filled with demo tapes and handed the box to Keith. "That's Roy Dan Willson, with two Ls. You look for his name 'cause one of these days you'll be seeing it in platinum. Thanks for delivering these. The postage was killing me. And remember, you get a free sandwich and a free cup of coffee anytime you're in the neighborhood."

"I imagine I'll be seeing you frequently," said Keith. He smiled and tipped his hat and carried the box of tapes out the door to his rig.

Mama frowned when she saw Todd and R.J. playing with the sugar containers. "It's one o'clock in the morning. Don't those kids got a curfew? What are they doing here anyway?"

"They came to hear Daddy sing."

"Oh," said Mama, looking them over as if in a new light. "In that case, don't just stand there. Go see what they want."

I took their orders. All the while Cindy looked at me as if she wanted to say something, but she didn't. I could smell the liquor on Todd's breath. Daddy came in and played another set. Todd and the other boys clapped and yelled obnoxiously every time Daddy finished a song. He looked over at them in irritation, but Mama soaked it up. "Go over and give those kids more refills of soda." She didn't seem to notice they were stinking drunk. And they just kept acting drunker. I would have thought that the caffeine in the cola might have sobered them up.

Every time I went to their booth, I lingered awhile. Cindy kept looking at me as if she was a puppy in the back of a dogcatcher's truck. "Get me out of here," her eyes seemed to say.

That's when I saw it.

Todd had a bottle of whiskey concealed in his coat pocket. I noticed it when he poured some liquor into his Coke.

My heart raced. A million thoughts swirled through my head. What would Mama do if she saw the bottle? What would Daddy do? What if Todd got in a wreck driving home? What if he killed Cindy?

The next hour dragged on and Todd and the others got more and more obnoxious. They howled like dogs after every song Daddy sang. Daddy glared at them. Cindy kept looking at the door as if she wanted to spring to freedom. I hung around their booth trying to think of a way to get Cindy out of there.

It was a quarter to two. "Play that song you wrote for the café," said Mama.

"Yeah, Mr. Willson. Play us that song you wrote for the café. Bet you did a lot of writing in prison," mocked Todd. Cindy elbowed him, but it had no effect.

Daddy's eyes turned an icy blue and he just stared at Todd. Finally, Todd shut up and Daddy sang:

> There is pain in Comfort.
> There is comfort in pain.

But I find peace of mind at the Comfort Café.
Misery's at my shoulder.
Sorrow's my next of kin,
But they've grown to be familiar,
So I think of them as friends.
Take me home to where I belong.
Take me home though the road is long.
I'll make a bed of roses.
Lay me down in the grass.
'Til I find myself in Comfort at last.

The boys giggled during the song. Then, feeding off of each other's stupidity, they howled to the melody. Daddy set down his guitar when he'd finished, then stood up. If I could have read his mind, I would have guessed he was calculating how many years he'd get in Hondo for busting the guitar over Todd's head and whether or not it would be worth it.

"Don't stop now. Play us another song," wailed Todd. He seemed to have no realization that he might be treading into dangerous water.

"It's time to go, boys," said Daddy.

"Go on and play another set," coaxed Mama. "The kids wanna hear you play some more."

"I've had it," yelled Daddy. I couldn't tell if he was more exasperated with the boys or with Mama. "It's time for you kids to get on home. I'm going out back for a smoke. When I come back in, don't be here."

Daddy made a beeline for the back door. Mama followed him out. "But they love your singing," I heard her say as the back door closed.

"Come on, Todd, let's just leave," pleaded Cindy.

Get out, Todd, while the getting is good, I wanted to say.

"But we're having such a *good* time. Aren't we, baby?" Todd grabbed Cindy and pushed his lips into hers. Kissing her, I guessed, though it looked more like he was trying to suffocate her with his face.

Cindy pushed Todd away and slapped him. The others laughed. Todd got red in the face with embarrassment. He pushed Cindy, so hard that she hit her head against the wall behind the booth.

I had always feared that one day all of the anger inside of me would burst through the surface. It happened in that moment when I saw Todd push Cindy.

I didn't see anything for a moment but a flash of red. It was blinding. The next thing I knew I had grabbed Todd Anderson by his collar and literally yanked him to his feet. He stood a good ten inches taller than I did. Fortunately, I came back to reality in time to stop myself from leveling him.

"Don't you ever hit her again," I said.

"Don't, Kenny," said Cindy, rubbing the back of her head.

Todd looked back at the other boys and laughed. They laughed too, but they also looked nervous. Nobody stood up to Todd. Nobody.

He brushed my hands away as if they were pieces of lint on his clothing. Then he narrowed his eyes.

"You ever touch me like that again, I'll kill you." He sat back down in the booth next to Cindy. "Now get us some more soda. I'm thirsty."

I was shaking. I was scared. More scared than I'd ever been. More scared than Daddy and Mama put together could have ever made me. I was afraid of Todd. I was afraid of my anger. But at that moment I was angrier than I was scared. I leaned over Todd. "You ever touch her like that again, and I'll kill *you*. Get your own dang soda." I turned and walked away. Not a smart thing to do.

I felt the whiskey bottle hitting me in the back of the head. It fell to the ground about the same time that I did. Then Todd pulled me up by the collar. He raised his fist, about to punch me in the face.

"Stop it, Todd," I heard Cindy scream.

What happened next occurred so quickly that I barely saw what happened. Daddy grabbed Todd's wrist, spun him around, and pinned him to the wall with his hand on Todd's throat.

"You ever killed anybody, boy?" Daddy asked Todd.

Todd tried to shake his head, but Daddy had such a grip on his neck that all he managed was a few short jerks.

The three girls and two boys watching looked fearful. I wondered if they were thinking what I was thinking. Had my daddy ever killed anybody? We all knew he'd committed armed robbery, but was he a killer?

"There's a place about here," Daddy squeezed Todd's neck and Todd screamed. "If you apply enough pressure, you can crush a person's windpipe and they suffocate to death real quick."

I saw terror in Todd's eyes. I felt a rush of panic. *Would Daddy actually kill him?*

"What's going on?" Mama said, walking into the room.

Daddy let go of Todd's neck. "Todd and I were just discussing whether these kids were gonna stay or whether they were gonna leave."

"I think we're about ready to leave," said Todd hoarsely. He rubbed his throat. The other kids quickly nodded their heads in agreement.

"What's this?" said Mama, picking up a piece of the broken whiskey bottle and looking at me in accusation.

"It isn't mine," I said, glaring at Todd.

Jake pulled up in his patrol car and strode inside just as Todd and the others were putting on their coats. He looked from me to Daddy as I cleaned up the shattered glass. Then he looked at Todd, as if he was sizing up the situation.

I saw panic in Mama's eyes. Daddy, the law, and whiskey all in the same room were not a good combination. But Jake didn't say anything about the liquor. He walked over to Cindy.

"Cindy, you got thirty seconds to get out to my car so I can get you home before your daddy gets there. And if you're lucky, I can talk him out of the switching he's planning on giving you. He's been looking for you for two hours." Jake glanced at Todd in disapproval. "You were supposed to be home by twelve."

"I know," said Cindy. "I'm sorry." She hurried out to Jake's car.

The sheriff studied the boy's bloodshot eyes. "Give me your keys," he finally said to Todd.

"But I —" Todd started to protest.

"Don't wear my patience, son," said Jake.

Todd handed over his keys.

"You girls get in the patrol car."

The other two girls hurried outside.

"You boys can walk home."

"But it's a mile to my house," whined R.J.

"The fresh air will do you good." Jake left and drove the girls to their homes. The boys shrugged their shoulders and started walking.

"Your friends are trouble," said Mama, as if I was responsible for them.

Unfortunately I had no idea just how much trouble Todd was going to be.

chapter 10

It was four weeks later, the third weekend in April. We were getting on the bus at seven o'clock on a Friday morning, all of us in Mrs. Peterson's journalism class. Heading to the Regional University Interscholastic League Competition over in San Marcos. Twenty girls and me. Not a bad ratio.

Mama was pretty hot about having to give me two whole days off from the café, but I needed it. It turned out that we now got ninety percent of our customers between 2 and 6 A.M., after the bars closed. Daddy had become a hot number in Comfort and I was one dead-tired indentured servant. Mama kept promising me that things were going to get better when "Daddy made it big," but I wasn't holding my breath waiting for that to happen. It was one thing to be big in Comfort. It was quite another to be big in the larger scope of the world.

"Come sit with me, kid," said Cindy, planting a kiss on the top of my head. I followed her to the back of the bus. Her short, dark hair bounced as she walked.

Cindy and I had been avoiding each other at school. There was an unspoken pact between us not to anger Todd. Cindy still sat with him at lunch. She still laughed at his stupid jokes. *How could she do that after the way he'd treated her?*

I wondered who the real Cindy was. The one I knew or the one she showed to the rest of the school?

Cindy slid onto the very last black vinyl seat. It was a brand-new bus, all shiny and yellow outside. Black and clean inside. I just stood there in the aisle, breathing in how good the rubbery smell felt in my nostrils. I was afraid to sit down. I suddenly had the awful thought that maybe I'd been hallucinating and Cindy hadn't really asked me to join her.

She looked up at me, smiled, and patted the seat. "Aren't you gonna sit down, silly?"

"Oh yeah," I said, sliding next to her but trying not to get too close. "I was just sniffing the bus."

She threw back her head and laughed. I realized how stupid I sounded. "Sniffing the bus. Kid, you kill me."

Then she got real quiet and she did something that nearly gave me a heart attack. She wove her arm through mine and held my hand, real tight, as if she was hanging on for her life. She looked right into my eyes and she whispered, "Kenny, why can't all the boys be like you?"

"Francesca Adams," called out Mrs. Peterson from where she was standing at the front of the bus.

"Here," said Francesca.

I stared straight ahead at Mrs. Peterson to avoid responding to Cindy's question. It wasn't the sort of thing a person could really answer, anyway.

"Kenny Willson," called Mrs. Peterson.

"Here," I said, but I wondered if I really was, because Cindy was still holding my hand and my head felt as if it was somewhere in outer space.

The bus drove through the rolling, green hills. When most people think of the state, they think of west Texas with its miles of flat farmland, its dust storms, and its dry, parched heat. South central Texas isn't like that at all. It's more like New Orleans with its humidity and lush green vegetation. Even its music.

The bluebonnets had just started to bloom and I tried counting them to take my mind off of Cindy as she put her other hand on my arm and squeezed my elbow. The bus was only half full so there wasn't anybody near us, which was good. I didn't want anybody talking to Todd and shortening my life expectancy.

"Todd wants me to do it," said Cindy, after a long period of silence.

"It?" I asked stupidly.

"You know."

There was "it" with a lower-case *i*, which could mean anything. Then there was "It" with a capital *I*, which could only mean one thing. I didn't understand why "It" should be considered part of the prom package.

"Why?" I asked, even more stupidly.

She rolled her eyes.

"I mean, you're not going to."

[99]

She looked out the window. "He said he loves me, but he has needs. He said I'm not taking care of him. He said he still wants to go with me, but maybe he should start sleeping around. It wouldn't mean anything. Just to take care of his needs. He says we'll both go off to college and we should do it at least once before we leave. He says, 'How much fun will the prom be if all we do is dance?' And I do believe he loves me in his own way."

It sounded to me as if Todd's "way" involved using every argument he could think of to get what he wanted.

I'll admit that Todd held a certain charm for just about every girl at Comfort High. But how someone as smart and wonderful as Cindy Blackwell fell for a clod like Todd was beyond me. Then I recalled that she'd started dating him after my article calling him the "Steam Roller of Comfort High." I had written that he moved like "a fine machine, *poetry* in motion."

A sick feeling settled in my stomach and I felt responsible. "But if he loves you, he shouldn't want to be with anybody else."

"That's exactly what he said. 'I love you. I don't want to be with anybody else. But I have these needs. . . .'" Her voice trailed off. She and I both knew Todd could snap his fingers and have girls lining up halfway to Amarillo.

"But you're not going to. I mean, you're better than that. You're better than he is. Make him wait. He'll wait," I lied.

She looked away and started crying. Then I saw something in her eyes that told me that even though her brain, her experience, and her logic said that Todd was a swine, her heart had told her something different.

"I thought maybe I loved him," she said. "I thought maybe it would be nice."

Then I remembered how she'd looked as if she'd been crying that night at the café and I realized she'd already done It. The thought of his fat hands on her made me want to puke. I couldn't look at her. I turned toward the aisle and hung my head.

I guess she took it wrong because she pulled her arm away from mine. "Do you think I'm a slut now?"

"God, no. I just can't stand the thought of him . . ." I couldn't say it.

She was crying again.

Then I did something stupid. I put my arm around her. She buried her head in my shoulder and cried harder. Girls were looking. I didn't care. I was mad. It wasn't what Todd had done so much as the sleazy way he'd done it. The way he'd made her feel cheap. Todd could pulverize me if he wanted to. I was pissed off enough to go down fighting, making him sorry for the way he'd treated her.

But first things first. Win the regionals, go to state, win the money. . . .

Get Cindy and me both out of Comfort.

chapter 11

We arrived in San Marcos early that Friday morning but as it turned out, all of my events were scheduled for Saturday. Cindy, Francesca, and I spent that first day playing chess and swimming in the hotel pool.

The next morning I was up early. My plan was to finish the newswriting and sportswriting competitions, then conveniently get sick so I didn't have to participate in the poetry reading. Mary Jane Johnson, the alternate, had been standing around all day with nothing to do. She'd be thrilled if she could compete in my place.

I completed the newswriting competition and felt pretty good about it. Thirty kids sitting in a classroom. A judge, a timer, a piece of paper listing all the relevant facts that needed to be included in the story. We received a pencil, two blank pieces of paper, one for the rough draft of the story and one for the final copy. I was pretty nervous, but now I felt relaxed. Now I was ready for the thing I was really good at . . . sportswriting. There was a thirty-minute break between events. I sat outside the room where they would be holding the sportswriting competition and ate a Snickers bar. A bunch of nervous girls and a boy with glasses as thick as Coke bottles fluttered around outside the door. This was going to be easy. There was no way these kids could write about football the way I wrote about football. They hadn't run with the pigskin clutched to their chest or felt the icy chill of frozen air terrorizing their lungs as they tried to sprint for the goal and dodge a tackle named Tractor in the cold night air.

The door opened and we poured into the room. The moderator, a woman in a brown skirt and flat shoes, stood at the door, making sure nobody took anything inside the room. I chose a seat near the front where I could keep a good eye on the clock so as to gauge my time. When everyone was seated, the moderator passed out pencils and blank pieces of paper. Then she passed out green pieces of paper with the story information outlined on it and laid them facedown on everyone's desk.

"Do not turn these papers over until you are instructed to do so," said the woman, her mouth pinched in a severe and official sneer.

The boy with bifocals let out a gasp. I couldn't help but wonder what he was thinking. Was he afraid he'd accidentally turn the paper over too soon and get a thrashing?

I'd already worked out some ideas in my head about what to include in the story. If the event was football I'd put in something about the feeling of cleats digging into the grass.

If it was basketball, I'd write about the way the court vibrates with the echo of the ball bouncing across the wooden floor.

"Go," said the moderator.

I turned over my paper and looked at the subject line: "Middlefield High School Chess Tournament."

SATURDAY, APRIL 5.

Billy James advanced to the quarterfinals of the state chess championship after beating Meredith Whatley, a student of Binford High. During the semifinals, Billy had Jason Cort, the previous state champion, in check after only three moves. At the final round, Billy James took on Connie Wong in a game that lasted two and a half hours. He finally cornered her with a pawn and a rook and took the game.

I had played chess on only two occasions, at the insistence of Cindy, who beat me pretty quick both times. I felt my upper lip sweating. I looked over at the boy with the glasses. He smiled and wrote as fast as his fingers would let him.

Mrs. Peterson always told us, "Don't just sit there staring at the paper because the only thing that's going to happen is that it's going to stare right back at you. Write something. Anything."

So this is how I started my rough draft. *Chess sucks.* Then

I couldn't think of anything else to say, so I wrote it again. *Chess sucks.* Then I wrote it about a hundred more times. By then we only had twenty minutes left and I was nervous. It shouldn't be that hard, I told myself. But those cold facts just kept staring at me. I couldn't think of a single way to put them together into a meaningful whole. In middle school I once had to write a story about Suzie Blackwell, Cindy's younger sister. She'd won the long jump competition at the district track meet. What's there to say about the long jump? You run and you jump and you fall in the sand. But it was a big deal because we hadn't won a single track event that year. I wasn't even there. The coach handed me a program with some notes written on it. I started that story five different times but it kept sounding like an advertisement for dry cereal. Finally, I decided to try two things. First, I imagined it was Cindy jumping across the sand with those long, pelican legs, instead of just her short, scrawny sister. Second, I put it in the context of football instead of track. I ended up saying something about Suzie sailing to her goal right over the heads of the defense, suspended in the splits, hanging in midair. I got a note from the assistant principal regarding the "questionable content" of my article. Then Suzie started following me around like a stray looking for a home.

I could do it again. I could make chess exciting. And by the time I was finished I would not only win first place, I'd have the judges dying to play chess. I might even get myself excited about chess.

> *Billy James looked into the eyes of Connie Wong. He could smell blood. It was his. "I ain't going down without a fight," he told her, as he tucked the pawn under his arm and ran like a smiling jackass toward his goal. "Get outta my way you bastards," he screamed as he sprinted past the Knights, wove in and out between them black-jersied Castles, jumped over the head of the Queen, until he arrived at the ten-yard line. He smiled at the Rook, gave him the signal, then they closed in for the massacre.*

That was it. I had exactly two minutes left to rewrite the story in my school voice.

I never much thought of myself as a writer until I got involved in Mrs. Peterson's journalism class. I realize I talk like a hick. I don't have much regard for grammar, and looking words up in the dictionary does nothing but confuse me. I never understand the words Webster's uses to explain the word I'm looking up, so I get four more words I need to look up to understand the first one and by that time I get so frustrated I want to throw the darn book against the wall. But with Mrs. Peterson I learned to do something I call translation. She calls it rewriting, but it's really a translation, because first I write a story in my thinking and talking voice. Then I have to take out all the "ain'ts" and cuss words, if there are any, and write it in my school voice.

I had just finished rewriting the story in my school voice when the timer buzzed. Read it and weep, judges, I thought to myself.

I had an hour-and-a-half break before the preliminary poetry-reading competition. I planned on feigning my pretend illness just before the event so I wouldn't have time to recuperate or be sent to a nurse to get checked out.

I walked over to the room where they were posting the winners for the newswriting competition. I checked the list. *First Place—Jones, Eli; Second Place—Kitt, Ty; Third Place—Hammer, Jay; Alternate—Sweeney, Sue.* I felt my heart sink when I didn't see my name, but I told myself it was okay because I knew I'd knocked the judges away with my sports story. Winning three hundred dollars at state for one event was all I needed, but that three hundred was essential to my plan.

The first three students to place would be going to the state competition in Austin in two weeks. The fourth-place winner could go as an alternate but could only compete if one of the other three couldn't make it for some reason.

"Kenny," I heard someone squeal behind me. Francesca Adams, who had already won the spelling bee, came running up behind me. "Did you hear? Cindy won first place for editorial writing." Cindy came walking up with a medal hanging around her neck. She twisted it up to the light. "What do you think? Pretty cool, huh." Her eyes were beaming. I was glad to see that all the sadness was gone. Maybe she would forget about Todd altogether. She leaned over and whispered in my ear, "Now I can tell my daddy to shove it. I don't have to go to that secretarial school in San Antonio."

I couldn't imagine Cindy or anybody else telling Buddy Blackwell to shove it. He owned a Ford lot over on Highway 27 and one day when the president of the First State Bank wouldn't give one of his customers a car loan due to questionable credit, Mr. Blackwell drove a truck through the front door of the bank. He claimed in court that it was an accident due to a malfunction in the brake mechanism. Nobody quite believed him but the item was on recall due to similar incidents, so Mr. Blackwell got off. After that the First State Bank never failed to grant a car loan to any of Buddy Blackwell's customers.

"I'm going to Texas Women's University in Denton."

My heart raced as I imagined Cindy dumping Todd and running away with me to Dallas when I hit the road that summer. I *had* to win the sportswriting event. I needed that cash prize.

If you go to the state UIL competition, even if you don't win at that level, there are hundreds of different scholarships you can apply for. There was a real possibility that Cindy could get enough money to do whatever she pleased. Of course, standing up to her daddy was gonna be a whole other matter. Nobody was going to help her with that one.

Dr. and Mrs. Adams walked over to us.

"Congratulations, girls," said Mrs. Adams.

"We'll see you later, honey," said Dr. Adams, kissing his daughter's cheek. "We're going to get something to eat. You win any medals yet?" said Dr. Adams, turning to me.

"I think I did pretty good in my last event, but they haven't announced the places yet."

"Keep up the good work," said the doctor. "I expect to see all three of you in Austin."

"Yes, sir," I said.

"Let's go to the Dairy Queen and celebrate," said Francesca after her parents left.

There was still an hour before the poetry competition, so we walked across the street and I bought myself a basket of chicken fingers. Cindy didn't have anything but a Coke and a salad but Francesca ate like a cow. She had two burgers, a dilly bar, then she ordered extra fries and swirled them around in her vanilla shake.

I figured that right after lunch would be a good time to feign my imaginary illness.

"You're going to make me puke," said Cindy, watching Francesca consume the fries dripping with ice cream. "How can you eat like that?"

"Track," said Francesca. The girl had thighs the size of a

running back's, which is where I guess she put all those fries because the rest of her was flat and skinny.

We walked back across the street. It was about time for the officials to post the winners for the sportswriting contest. "Congratulations, Elmer," I heard a girl say to the boy with the bifocals. I tried to squeeze up to the table where the places were posted, but there were too many people in front of me. The crowd finally thinned and I pushed my way to the front and read: *First Place—Swisher, Elmer; Second Place—Smith, Ann; Third Place—Pole, Kate; Alternate—Handy, Luke.*

I read it again. That couldn't be right. I read it a third time. I hadn't won diddle. I wasn't even the alternate.

Cindy walked up and grabbed my arm. "Where you been, kid? You weren't in the preparation room. They already announced that we're starting with the diversity category for the prelims. Come on, or we're gonna be late for the preliminary round." Cindy started pulling me toward the hallway.

"No!" I pulled away from her in a panic. I was supposed to be in the bathroom, pretending to have food poisoning.

"What's wrong?" asked Cindy.

A thousand thoughts swirled through my head. On the one hand, there was no way I could get up in front of those judges and recite another poem. On the second hand, it was my last chance to go to state, win the money, and spend the rest of my life with Cindy. On the third hand, there was no way I could win the poetry reading if I got up in front of everybody and peed my pants. On the fourth hand . . .

"Are you upset about not placing in sportswriting?" Cindy asked.

"Among other things," I said. "I can't recite those poems, Cindy. You saw what happened last time."

"I saw that you won third place."

"I'm nervous," I said, not wanting to use the true adjectives—"petrified," "terrified," and "paralyzed."

"Get over it," she said, taking me by the hand and leading me off to another room. The last thing I wanted to do was read some danged poem about my "unconquerable soul."

As I followed her down the hall I felt as if I was being led to my execution. But I didn't get my last meal, I wanted to say.

We squeezed into a large lecture room. All the chairs were taken so we sat on the floor.

The longer I sat there, the more nervous I got. What if in addition to my throat not working, my legs quit on me and I couldn't even walk up to the podium?

I felt my pulse quickening.

When they finally called my number, I somehow managed to stand up. As I walked to the podium, I noticed that I couldn't feel my legs. It was like an out-of-body experience. I stood up in front of everybody. This time the panic attack started immediately. "Run . . . run . . . run . . ." said the voice in my head.

"You can do it," mouthed Cindy.

Then I considered the fact that even though the last reading was disastrous, I hadn't died from it. I figured I wouldn't die this time either. I opened my black folder and stuck my nose in it so I wouldn't have to look at the judges. I decided to start with the shortest poem. I did not breathe. I did not pause. I did not stop to emphasize punctuation for poetic effect. "Out of the night that covers me, Black as the spit from pole to pole, I thank whatever gods may be for my unconquerable soul . . ."

I had the vague sense that I sounded like a cattle auctioneer, and I could have sworn I used the word "spit" instead of "pit."

At that moment I didn't think about Dallas or the state championship in Austin. All I wanted was to survive the next five minutes. I read my other poems pretty much the same way.

When I sat down all Cindy said was, "Interesting interpretation, kid." She had a funny look in her eye, almost as if she were serious.

I couldn't believe it when they announced that I made it to the final round. Cindy made it too, but of course, that was a given.

"Why me?" I asked Cindy. "Don't those judges have some kind of standards?"

"You've got passion, Kenny. That counts for a lot."

"But didn't you hear me say 'Black as the *spit* from pole to pole?'"

"No."

"No? How could you miss it?"

Cindy squeezed my shoulder. "Kenny, relax. You always sound worse to yourself than you do to others."

"Really?" I hadn't considered that.

I spent the next hour losing miserably at chess. I was so nervous that my intestines felt as if they'd been ripped out of my gut and run over by a semi truck.

But Cindy Blackwell had said that I had passion.

Somehow I would work up the nerve I needed for the final round.

We went back to the lecture room and I waited for my turn. When my name was called I walked up to the podium. Cindy flashed me a smile and I knew I would be all right.

But that was before I opened my notebook. As I turned to the first poem I realized that it was upside down.

I looked at Cindy in panic. I knew I couldn't turn the notebook right-side up. My performance had to be flawless.

What would I do? I wondered if I could recite the poems from memory.

I cleared my throat and tried to begin my introduction. But I couldn't remember my introduction. I couldn't remember my poets' names. Heck, I couldn't even remember *my* name.

"What do a Massachusetts farmer, an English playwright, and

a one-legged pirate all have in common?" I stammered. I didn't mean for it to but I suddenly realized that my introduction sounded like a bad joke. Besides that, I'd jumbled up my categories.

"Hope!" I screamed out, trying to redeem myself.

Cindy looked at me and winced.

"I mean, what do any of us have in common? We have our dreams. Our visions may all be different, but that's what makes us human. The ability to dream."

I was dying up there. I couldn't stand it. I buried my nose in my notebook, even though I couldn't read the upside-down words, and I recited my poems as fast as I could. Then I walked out of the room without looking back.

I won fourth place in the poetry-reading contest. Who would have guessed? Cindy won first. I was only an alternate, but in two weeks I'd be on my way to Austin, Texas, and the state championship.

I'd get to spend the day with Cindy, but I wouldn't be able to compete, which was probably a good thing. I'd have to figure out another way to get the extra money I needed for Dallas.

chapter 12

Mama was irritated that I had taken the two days off to go to the competition in San Marcos. The fact that I won fourth place upset her more because she knew I'd be going to Austin in a few weeks for the state competition. I'd hoped she'd be proud. I guess that was too much to wish for. But just once I would have loved to hear her say, "Kenny, you done good."

It was Monday morning and it was raining, so things were slow. School had been canceled because of a stock show.

I felt sorry for Roy junior, staring at me from his mesh prison, so I took him out and set him on my knee and read to him from my English book. We were studying poets of the twentieth century.

Mama took a blue satin shirt out of a bag under the register and started sewing some white fringe around the buttons.

"Morning, Kenny," Jake said as he came in from outside. He'd started hanging around the café a little more and I was glad. He walked straight to the coffeepot and started to pour himself a cup, then saw that it was empty.

"There isn't any coffee," Jake hollered to Mama, who was busy working on the shirt.

"Just pour some water back over them grounds," she told him over her shoulder.

He grumbled and took a pitcher over to the sink. "The service around here isn't worth a darn, Maggie."

"It won't kill you to make a pot of coffee. I swear, the way you carry on," Mama told him.

I smiled to myself whenever they talked to each other this way, as if they were two married people who'd been together for years. Then I felt guilty for thinking like that. Daddy had been trying real hard to make a fresh start.

Mama picked up the blue shirt and showed it to Jake and me. She'd added rhinestones and fringe on the cuffs. "What do you think?" I didn't know what to say. She seemed so proud and the shirt was so darn ostentatious. I couldn't say "ostentatious," or what it meant—"pretentious," because Mama would have called me "affected," for using "high fal-lutin'" words.

"I thought Elvis was dead," said Jake. He had a way of cutting right to the truth of something.

Mama pouted. "I made it for Roy. To sing in."

"Scared me for a minute. Thought it might be for me," chuckled Jake.

Mama snapped him on the butt with a towel.

"Ouch. Didn't anyone ever tell you a body can pop out an eye that way?"

"I don't think you got eyes down there. Now shut up and go check the Crock-Pot. I got chili cooking for Frito pie."

Things were still slow and Roy junior had gone back to the playpen for a nap so I set myself a chair up in the corner and commenced to catch a little catnap. I was right in the middle of dreaming about Cindy Blackwell when I felt something sting the right side of my neck. It hurt like fire. I cried out in pain and covered my neck with my hand.

I looked up to see Mama standing there holding a dish-towel. She'd just hit me with it. I couldn't believe it. She could have hit me in the face. Not to mention the humilia-tion of being treated like a dog in a room full of people. "Kenny, what are you doing, sleeping? We got customers."

I felt rage bubbling to the surface again. It was getting harder and harder to keep a lid on it. I wanted to tear out her hair. Then I was afraid and ashamed of how angry I felt. If I didn't leave soon, someday I would do something I'd regret. Next time it wouldn't be a car I was busting up.

She turned and walked off and it's a good thing she didn't stick around because I stood up and clenched my fists. I could feel how red and hot my face had become, which first made me angry then ashamed because one of the customers sitting at the bar was Cindy Blackwell.

"You shouldn't treat the boy like that," I heard Jake tell Mama.

"Like what?"

"Popping him in the face."

Cindy's head was cradled in her folded arms so I didn't think she saw what happened. I hoped she hadn't heard either.

Mama studied me, as if to see if there was any merit to Jake's words. I was still clenching my fists. I didn't want her seeing how mad she'd made me so I looked away. She walked back over, put an arm around me, and sat next to me in a booth while Jake put a lid on his coffee and left.

Don't touch me, I wanted to scream.

"I guess I been riding you pretty hard, what with the café being open all night. Something big is gonna happen for your daddy soon. I can feel it."

"Dallas, Dallas, Dallas, Dallas," I said to myself, under my breath to keep from ripping her head off. If she was going to be mean, why not just stay mean all the time? It was her momentary lapses into kindness that got to me more than anything else. I pictured myself getting on the bus with Cindy and my shoe box full of money. "Dallas, Dallas, Dallas, Dallas," I said as Mama walked back into the kitchen and I was finally able to relax my fists.

I walked over and sat down on a stool next to Cindy. She still had her head down, which was a little odd. Maybe she'd fallen asleep, I thought. "Hey," I said.

Cindy looked up. She'd been crying, and a nasty black bruise covered her eye and half her face.

"My God. What happened to you?"

"My daddy hit me," she said softly. Then, turning her face to the seven or eight people in the café, she yelled, "My daddy hit me. Mr. Buddy T. Blackwell from Buddy's Cars. He punched me right in the face, the SOB."

People stopped eating and talking and stared at her uneasily. I grabbed her hand. "Shh, Cindy, you don't want everyone knowing your business."

"Yes I do," she yelled even louder. "Buddy T. Blackwell is a child beater. I'm telling everybody I see. Maybe if people know what he is, he'll be ashamed and leave us alone."

It was no secret that Buddy Blackwell had, on more than one occasion, sent his wife to the hospital with a fractured wrist or rib or a broken collarbone. I guessed he took a belt to his kids on occasion, but I had no idea he would actually punch a girl in the face.

A trucker entered and made a beeline for the register. "Hey, you!" Cindy hollered at him.

The man stopped and looked behind him, thinking she must be talking to someone else. "See this eye? Buddy T. Blackwell is a child beater."

The man looked at the floor in embarrassment and hurried over to the register.

Cindy lay her head back down on the counter and let the tears flow. People were watching. I didn't care. For the second time in a week I put my arm around her.

Mama walked over from the register after the trucker paid for his gas. "We got other customers that need waiting on. She's making a scene. Tell her to go on home."

"Mama," I said, "jump in the deep fryer."

"What did you say to me?" she snapped. She might hit me. I didn't care. She'd already struck out at me once that morning.

"Come on, Cindy. Let's get out of here."

I took Cindy's hand and led her out back, where we sat down on a couple of milk crates.

She buried her head on my shoulder and cried. I didn't know what to do so I just sort of patted her hair as if she was a kitten.

Then she put her arms around me and nuzzled my neck with her nose.

By then my hands were dangling stupidly at my sides. I still didn't know what to do with them so I just perched them on her waist while I thought about where they should go. I hoped it wasn't too disrespectful.

That seemed to be okay with her because she stopped crying and didn't whack me. So I sort of eased my hands up her back and rested them on her shoulders.

Then I did something so stupid it was beyond ignorance.

I kissed her cheek.

Then she kissed me back.

On the mouth.

It was a wet, open kiss.

I opened my mouth and let her. I kept my eyes open too, because I expected to be shot at any minute by Todd Anderson or Buddy Blackwell.

She kept kissing me, and finally I closed my eyes and just thought about how good she tasted—a mixture of cola and strawberry lip-gloss.

Finally she stopped and I fell backward onto the milk crates. I must have looked a fool because she covered her mouth with her hand and giggled at me.

"You kiss me, then you laugh," I said, teasing her.

"You have lipstick on your face," she smiled.

I used my shirttail to wipe my face, and sure enough, red lipstick came off.

Cindy's eyes got sad again and she said, "I love you, kid."

Then she turned and ran back to her car, crying.

I couldn't get up. I just lay there on the milk crates wondering if I had just had a hallucination. Either that or I'd died and gone to heaven. She had kissed me. She had said she loved me. Did that really happen?

The future suddenly became very clear in my mind. Cindy would dump Todd Anderson. After all, she didn't love him. She loved me. She and I would run away to Dallas. I needed at least three hundred more dollars. No, I'd need more than that if Cindy were going with me. I couldn't count on winning the UIL money, but Mama had been getting more and more distracted with sending Daddy's tapes off to Nashville. I could probably dip a little deeper into the till without her noticing. Cindy didn't need her crappy family any more than I needed mine. I could just picture the look on her face when I told her I was going to get her out of town.

Grandpa Harris was going to love Cindy.

I finally stood up and brushed myself off. I looked in the

side mirror of the pickup to make sure my face was clean. Then I walked back into the café. Actually, I floated back inside.

"Yo, Kenny," I heard a voice say. I turned to see Todd Anderson sitting at one of the tables with R.J. and Petey. I wondered what they were doing there. They should have all been at the stock show.

He waved me over. I froze where I was. I couldn't move. I was surprised that my legs even continued to hold me up. Jake had left and the only other person in the dining room besides me and the boys was an old trucker.

All I could do was imagine how my blood was going to look, splattered all over the black-and-white linoleum floor after Todd bashed in my head. *Kenny, clean up that blood,* I could imagine Mama saying.

"Come here!" Todd's voice had that angry, forceful tone that nobody ever dared to ignore. The thought occurred to me to sprint as fast as I could out the back door, but I knew he'd catch up to me. Besides, I was probably safer getting beat up in the café, where at least somebody could call the law.

I slowly shuffled my feet toward him. I thought about Cindy's lips on mine and wondered if kissing her was worth getting killed over.

Yeah, it was. I quickly tucked in the lipstick-stained tail of my shirt.

"Sit down." Todd pulled out a chair.

"Can't. I gotta work."

"Where you been?" asked Todd.

"Nowhere." I wondered if he could hear that my voice was shaking. I knew from experience that there was nothing I could do to keep it from trembling.

"The question is, who you been *with?*" asked R.J., chuckling.

I felt my face turn hot. "Nobody!" What had they seen?

"Then what's that on your neck?" asked Petey.

I covered my neck with my hand. I didn't remember Cindy kissing me on the neck. I ran into the bathroom and looked in the mirror. There was a red mark left from where Mama popped me with the towel. It looked like a huge hickey.

Todd, R.J., and Petey came into the bathroom. They were blocking my way out. There was no other means of escape. I was at their mercy.

R.J. howled. "Kenny's got himself a girl!"

"No I don't," I said in the middle of a full-blown panic attack.

"No use denying it. We can see the evidence," said Petey.

I looked around the bathroom. There was one urinal and one stall. Maybe I could run into the stall and lock the door. No. I had once seen Todd get mad and dismantle a refrigerator sitting out in the alley with his bare hands.

It occurred to me that Todd had the physical ability to kill me if he wanted to. This time his judgment was not impaired with alcohol and there was no Daddy around to rescue me.

"You seen Cindy?" asked Todd.

"Cindy? Cindy who?" I moved backward toward the stall. Todd walked over and grabbed me by the shoulder, hard. All I could think about was how easily he could break my neck with that hand. My daddy had instructed him how.

"Don't give me that crap. Tell me where she is!"

R.J., all the humor gone from his voice, patted Todd on the back. "Ease up, Todd. He hasn't seen her."

Todd let go of my shoulder and punched the side of the bathroom stall so hard that his fist left a dent and the door came loose from its hinges. "Damn!" He sat on the sink and covered his face with his hands. He was upset. Really upset. But all I could think about was how the weight of him was going to pull the sink out of the wall and how I'd have hell to pay from Mama over it. Of course, I'd be getting off easy if that were the worst thing about to happen.

"Cindy's in trouble," said R.J.

"Trouble? What kind of trouble?" I said, suddenly forgetting my own fear.

"What kind do you think?" said Petey.

"The same kind of trouble that got Luanne Waters sent to that special school for wayward girls," said R.J. "And her dad won't give her the money to take care of it. Says they're Catholic and she'll go to hell."

My head was spinning. *What were they saying? The money to take care of what?* Then it dawned on me.

"Cindy's pregnant," I said.

"Good, Einstein," said R.J. "You get an A for Human Growth and Development."

"Don't be a jerk, R.J.," said Todd. "We need his help."

Cindy was pregnant and she'd gone to her dad to ask for money for an abortion. That had to take some guts.

That's why he'd whacked her in the eye.

And it was all because of Todd Anderson. I looked at the dent he'd put in the bathroom stall. I looked at the way the sink was starting to pull out of the wall under the weight of his butt.

"Get off the sink," I said. I was surprised how quickly anger alleviated my fear.

"What?" he replied, looking up at me in disbelief.

"Get your butt off the sink before you pull it out of the wall," I said. R.J. and Petey looked from me to Todd for his reaction. He glared at me, thinking. Then he hopped off the sink, smiled, and slapped my cheek lightly as if I was an ornery younger brother.

"Cindy likes you. You gotta talk to her," said Todd.

"Me?"

"Tell her to do the right thing. Her daddy has her scared she's gonna burn for all eternity," said Todd. "You gotta convince her otherwise. Tell her she's gotta get rid of it."

"You want *me* to tell her to get rid of it?" I couldn't believe what they were asking me to do. It was preposterous.

"You blast through everybody's life, Todd, and you don't care what kind of mess you leave behind."

He didn't even react. He just continued to smile at me as if I was trying to punch him in the gut to prove how strong I was. It had no effect.

"Don't forget the money," said R.J.

"Oh yeah," said Todd. "She needs three hundred dollars to take care of it. None of us got that kind of money."

"What are you saying?" I asked, feeling the knot in my stomach grow tighter each moment.

"Cindy needs your help," said R.J. "She's counting on you."

It didn't sound to me as if Cindy was counting on anybody. It sounded like Todd was the one who needed help. "Where do you expect me to get three hundred dollars?" I knew they didn't know about my shoe box.

What were they after?

"The café has all that money coming through. Couldn't you just borrow some? I'd pay you back. Or else you could report it missing. Don't you have insurance for things like that?" Todd asked.

"You want me to steal from the café for you?" His audacity was just amazing. He actually expected me to clean up his mess. If it wasn't for the fact that I knew Cindy was in trouble and alone, I would have knocked him out, then and there.

"You gotta help her," said Todd.

"I'll think about it," I said.

"Don't think too long," said Todd. "Meet me at the Bob-cat Stadium day after tomorrow." Then he and the others left.

I walked back out into the café. The lunch rush was over. Mama watched the boys pile into Petey's pickup while she wiped down the tables. "I don't like those boys, and that girl is nothing but trouble." She was starting to sound like a recording.

"Mama," I said, trying to keep my voice calm but not succeeding.

"What?" she barked in irritation.

"Dallas!!!" I screamed. Then I turned and ran out the front door. But suddenly Dallas seemed very far away.

chapter 13

It was Wednesday afternoon. I had to run in order to make it on time from gym class to sixth-period sophomore English. The seniors were in the hall showing off class rings and having their pictures taken.

I was never going to be one of them.

I know a lot of kids hate school. Some kids are even terrified of it. But for me, school was the one place I felt safe, the one place I could relax and let down my guard. There were no crazy, unpredictable people there who might pop me with a rag when I least expected it. Even Todd acted somewhat like a human being at school.

I slipped into my desk just as the bell rang. Mrs. Peterson, who taught English as well as journalism, wrote the words "American Poets" on the chalkboard. The class let out a collective groan. We'd already studied British poets, haiku, and the sonnets of Shakespeare. Everybody thought we'd just about exhausted the subject.

Mrs. Peterson opened her book while the other students grumbled. "Today we'll be looking at Robert Frost and his focus on landscape as a backdrop for his poetry."

Another groan.

Mrs. Peterson smiled. "And I want you all to pay close attention to the way he used his surroundings to create mood and atmosphere, because your assignment this week is to write a poem about the place where you live."

A *really* loud groan. This time I groaned too. I couldn't imagine anything remotely poetic about a greasy café with a dilapidated shack out back. Daddy's stucco job had started to peel off the metal siding and our house looked worse than ever.

Mrs. Peterson gave us fifteen minutes at the end of class to jot down poem ideas.

My daddy sings in a cowboy hat, while my mama sweats and fries the fat. I hate to rhyme. Don't think me callous. But I wish I was in Dallas.

I wadded up the paper, walked over to the trash can, and threw it away. As I walked back to my desk, Suzie Blackwell smiled at me. It occurred to me that maybe she thought I was in sophomore English because of her. The thought turned in my stomach like a greasy burrito with a chili side. Maybe she did have a pretty smile, like Daddy said, but every time she opened her mouth all I could think about was the rubber bands and wire of the braces she used to wear.

I sat back down in my chair and took out a clean sheet of notebook paper. I guess it was partly true that I was in sophomore English because of Suzie. The one similarity between her and her sister Cindy was that they both had brains. Suzie might even have had more brains. One day I heard her talking about how she'd tested out of freshman English and how she was going to take core classes instead of study hall so she could graduate in two years instead of four.

When Mama pulled me out of athletics earlier that year, I thought real hard about what Suzie had said. I tested out of the second semester of freshman English, then I took sophomore math instead of study hall. It wasn't that hard. By the time I was a sophomore, I could be taking junior classes. I figured that if I did that every semester plus took a couple of summer school classes, I could graduate a whole year early. That was my initial plan. But Mama had become so unbearable that I knew I wouldn't last another two years. Besides, it seemed pretty clear that me graduating wasn't high in her scheme of things.

I tried to write a few more lines of poetry but they were just as bad as the first set. My throat tightened as if someone had a chokehold on my neck. I coughed, hoping the feeling would pass. I didn't know whose hands I was thinking about, Mama's or Daddy's or maybe Todd Anderson's.

Suzie went up front to sharpen her pencil and when she passed my desk, she slipped me an envelope. The note inside read, "A present for you from the yearbook committee." Inside was a picture. It was a photo of me in my football uniform taken at the homecoming game, the night before Mama took me off the team. I had just scored the winning touchdown and I was riding high on the shoulders of the rest of the team. I remembered that night how I felt as if nothing could touch me. I thought I was invincible.

I was wrong.

I looked back at Suzie and smiled weakly. "Thanks," I said.

She smiled back without saying anything.

I looked out the window and saw it had started raining. The day was so warm and muggy, steam was actually coming up from the pavement where the rain hit it. It was one of those humid, lazy Texas afternoons where dogs and old men sit out on the front porch napping, watching life go by. One of those days that saps the will to live out of your veins. I looked across the room. A couple of girls had their heads on their desks and one boy in the back row was snoring. The place felt suffocating and oppressive, more from the barometric pressure than the heat.

I stared at my paper again, but my mind churned with the trouble Todd had gotten Cindy into. I hadn't slept for two nights, worrying about her. She was in a real jam and it poked at me like a burr under my skin. I wanted to run out of there and fix it, but what could I do? All I knew was that I couldn't just sit there, watching my own life tick by with the second hand on the big classroom clock. The ache in the pit of my stomach started creeping up my throat. I was afraid

I might puke. I jumped out of my seat and walked up to Mrs. Peterson's desk.

"I gotta go," I told her, choking on the words.

"Kenny, are you okay? You look pale."

"I gotta go," I said. I collected my books and walked out of the classroom. I walked down the hall, past the office without checking out, and down the highway toward the café.

I thought the fresh air would help revive me, but it didn't. For one thing, it wasn't fresh. It was warm and thick and it stuck to the sides of my lungs as I walked home in the rain.

When I got to the café I slipped into the house out back. I was glad to see that nobody was home. I went to the bed, got out my box of money, and counted it. Six hundred and fifty dollars. I counted out three hundred and put it into an envelope. I'd already decided to give Todd the money. I decided before he'd ever left the café. I guess I could have given it directly to Cindy, but I felt weird doing that, as if I might be pressuring her to do something she didn't want to do. As if I was somehow part of it all. No, I'd give the money to Todd. Better not to let Cindy know I had anything to do with any of this. I didn't want it to skew her opinion about running away with me when the time came to ask her.

That left me with three hundred and fifty dollars. I'd need six hundred and fifty dollars more before I left for Dallas. I'd need an additional three or four hundred if I were taking Cindy with me. I felt guilty about the abortion and my part in it and I wondered when Cindy was planning on doing it.

I wondered if she and I could survive the next week. I wondered if we'd ever make it to the state meet. What if something went wrong with the operation and she got sick or hurt?

I'd felt a change inside of me after the regional competition in San Marcos. I'd managed to hold my own, even though I was terrified. Sure, I knew I'd botched up my readings both there and at Johnson City. But I'd still managed to place. *What would happen if I actually sucked it up and did a halfway decent job?* Maybe I could win the five hundred dollars, then leave for Dallas from Austin. I'd be halfway there. But I dismissed the idea. Mrs. Peterson would get in a world of trouble if a student came up missing.

Besides, I'd never win the money. I was just an alternate.

The thought of Daddy's thick envelope filled with cash flashed through my mind. I figured he didn't really need it because he would never actually pay back Smitty. Besides, hadn't Daddy told me how he wished he could make things up to me? I wondered where he had hidden it.

I sealed my own envelope and put it in my pocket. Then I lay down on the couch, and in spite of a spring poking my ribs, I finally fell sleep. I dreamed of schemes for getting the extra money I needed, but every dream ended in me getting beat up or arrested or worse.

It was after five o'clock by the time I woke up. I jumped up from the couch and combed my hair as I ran out to the café. Mama would be plenty mad that I was late.

When I got to the kitchen I slipped the Roy's Place T-shirt on over my other shirt and started washing dishes. Mama was up front on the phone. Good thing the café was empty. Maybe she wouldn't notice my tardiness.

The phone conversation lasted quite a while. I carried a stack of clean coffee mugs up front.

"Yes sir . . . uh-huh . . . I understand." Mama hung up the phone. Something had happened. I could tell by the look on her face. I'd learned to read Mama's moods and gauge my own actions accordingly, but I couldn't quite figure out her eyes this time.

She picked up Roy junior from where he was playing on the floor, walked over, sat on a booth, and bounced him on her knee. Then she started crying uncontrollably, burying her face in Roy junior's hair.

I walked over cautiously. "Mama, are you okay?"

She looked up at me over her tear-soaked cheeks and laughed. At first it was just a giggle. Then she threw back her head and howled.

I didn't know what to make of it.

Mama jumped up from the booth, still holding Roy junior in her arms. She balanced him on one hip, hugged me with the other, and then started dancing around the café with both of us in her arms.

"Mama," I said as we bounced across the linoleum. "Are you okay?"

She stopped dancing and kissed me so hard I thought she would bruise my cheek. "Okay? Am I okay? Honey, we're gonna be rich." She threw Roy junior up in the air and caught him as he giggled in ecstasy.

"What are you talking about?" I asked.

"That was *Austin City Limits* on the phone. You got any idea who that is, Kenny?"

"A TV show?" I asked.

"*The* TV show," corrected Mama. "They got everybody from Willie Nelson to Stevie Ray Vaughan on that show. This is your daddy's big break."

"I don't know, Mama."

"They're coming here. *Here,* to do a live show starring *your daddy.*"

Mama hugged my neck and danced around again until she got winded, then she set down Roy junior and flopped in a chair, fanning herself with a menu. I sat down next to her. My stomachache was returning. I knew I should have felt excited, but my family just wasn't that lucky. Maybe you make your luck or maybe you find it, but we'd never been any good at either.

"They wanted him to come to Austin but I had to explain how he couldn't exactly leave the county just now. You got any idea what this means, honey?" She reached across the table and clasped my hands in hers. "It's the answer to all our prayers."

Her prayers maybe. Not mine. I remembered Kerrville.

"Everything's gotta be perfect," she continued. "We gotta repaint the inside of the café and wax the floors. Then we gotta make a new sign. And I want neon. Lots of neon."

I knew who would be repainting the walls and hanging a new sign. My throat tightened again. "When are they coming?"

"Next Thursday. A week from tomorrow." She jumped out of her seat. "I gotta get busy and call back all those agents and tell 'em *Austin City Limits* is doing a show here." She jumped up and hurried over to the phone.

"But I'm supposed to leave for the state UIL competition next Thursday night."

"You're just an alternate, Kenny. You can't compete. It won't kill you to miss it."

Just an alternate.

I looked at the clock to avoid looking at her and realized the time. "I gotta go. I gotta meet somebody," I told Mama. Then I ran out the front door before she could say otherwise.

I found Todd sitting in the bleachers of the Bobcat Stadium, where we had agreed to meet. Without his friends flanking him he looked smaller than usual, and he was nervous too. Very nervous. He ran his fingers through his hair. "You got the money?" he asked when I sat down next to him.

I took the envelope out of my pocket and dropped it on his lap.

He stuck it in his jeans, letting out a sigh of relief.

"Thanks. You're a good kid. I'll pay you back. I promise."

"Yeah, sure." I wasn't planning on losing any sleep waiting for that to happen.

Todd stood up and smiled awkwardly. "I'll be seeing you. You're okay. Cindy's lucky to have you for a friend." He added the last as if it were an afterthought. Then he left, taking my money with him.

I watched him get in his pickup and drive off. The rain had stopped, leaving a thick dullness that made me feel weary. The dullness hung over the town like a sheet over the face of a dead man. Nothing ever happened here. Nothing ever would. There were some things you just couldn't escape. People eased into their lives and once they settled, they never changed. Mr. Blackwell would keep on beating up Mrs. Blackwell. Todd would keep on stampeding through people's lives, and Mama would keep on being Mama. *Austin City Limits* wouldn't change that.

I was sick and tired of saying yes, when I wanted to scream no.

I took the photo of my last game out of my pocket. I could look out across the field and pick out the exact spot where Todd and the other guys had hoisted me up on their shoulders, then paraded me around like the king of the world. I remembered how it felt, too. Up there above everybody else wearing my football gear. Nobody could guess I was a scrawny freshman with holes in my jeans. That night I was a champion.

Nothing was ever going to feel that way again. Certainly not poetry.

I felt the place sucking at me like quicksand. If I didn't leave soon it was going to pull me under.

Forget the UIL, I told myself. *Get out now, while you still can.*

chapter 14

Friday morning I was in the kitchen of the café making my usual breakfast—jelly, chocolate syrup, and marshmallow cream, sandwiched between two strawberry Pop-Tarts. I could hear Mama up front talking on the phone, calling every "half-wit" agent and "no-good, no-account, phlegm-brained" record producer who had returned Daddy's demo tape without a favorable response. She gave them all a piece of her mind.

Roy junior looked at my breakfast concoction with a pitiful yearning in his eyes. I guessed Mama had forgot to feed him again in all her excitement over Daddy. His lower lip quivered as I started to take a bite.

"Here," I said, handing him my breakfast. "That's the last two Pop-Tarts. I hope you enjoy it."

He squealed and ran off into the dining room as he pulled apart the Pop-Tarts and licked off the chocolate.

"You remember a demo tape you got about a month ago? Singer by the name of Roy Dan Willson?" Mama told each person on the phone while I tried to find something else to eat. She sounded haughty and superior. Vindication was sweet. "Well, *Austin City Limits* is coming to do a show with Roy Dan Willson as the featured performer this coming Thursday night. What do you think of that? You want a piece of the action now? They say he's gonna be bigger than Randy Travis."

It was the same canned speech for every phone call. I nearly had it memorized before I'd even finished my corn dog. That's when I heard, "He's gonna be bigger than Randy—Oh dang it, Roy junior. You've wet all over yourself. Kenneeeeeey!"

I grabbed my books and ducked out the back door before Mama could corner me into diaper duty. I ran about a block, then slowed to a walk and finished my breakfast.

The closer the day of the performance came, the more unbearable Mama got. The floor wasn't shiny enough. The new neon sign wasn't bright enough. If I stepped to the right, she let me know I should have gone to the left. If I stepped to the left, she whacked me. I felt as if I was walking through a minefield, only the mines kept moving and they seemed to be following me.

And school was nothing but a waste of time. If I wasn't going to graduate, what was the point of going at all? I felt like a dying man when he looks around at the rest of the world and knows that everyone is going to go on living as usual without him.

That's when the Plan started growing in my mind. Mama was promoting the Big Night. She had posters up from Kerrville to Fredericksburg to San Antonio, but none in

Comfort or Boerne, where Daddy might see them. It looked like Mama wasn't going to tell him about the show until the lights came on.

The café would be bringing in a lot of money. I could take the money I needed all at once. Mama wouldn't miss it. She'd be too excited about Daddy making it big. I'd leave right away, maybe that night.

"Aren't you gonna tell him about *Austin City Limits*?" I asked her later.

"He'll just fret if he has time to think about it," she told me by way of an explanation. "These things make him nervous. So I'm waiting until the last possible minute to let him know. He'll be fine if he doesn't have time to mull it over. You'll see, Kenny."

Don't mind those people with the TV cameras, honey. We're just expanding to a new clientele.

Cindy needed to know the Plan so she could meet me in Dallas after the UIL competition. I'd give her the money for her bus ticket and arrange some way to meet up with her. The Plan was the only thing that kept me going. Otherwise I might have lost my mind.

But then every time I looked at Roy junior, I felt bad about running out on the kid. Sure, he was a pain, but I was all he had. I remembered being little like that and scared and not having anybody. It got to where I couldn't look him in the eye.

Mama was completely preoccupied with Daddy and

Daddy was completely preoccupied with his AA meetings. He went every day at noon, seven days a week. Fortunately, he found a ride with another man in the program so I didn't have to take him.

I tried to talk to Cindy at lunch that Friday but Todd stuck to her like glue. I worried about her. She looked tired and sick and far away. I had to let her know we needed to talk and I needed to do it soon. The Plan and the memory of the Kiss were all I had to hang onto. So I did something I wouldn't normally do. I wrote a note and gave it to her sister, Suzie, in sixth-period English class. Her eyes lit up when she saw me put the folded-up paper on her desk. "Give this to Cindy," I whispered. The lights went out and she frowned. "Please," I added.

"Okay," she said in disappointment, putting the paper in her assignment keeper.

Mrs. Peterson said as we were leaving, "Remember, your poems are due this Monday. They're to be about something in your immediate environment."

The poem was the least of my concerns.

When I got to the café that afternoon, Mama was still on the phone. I grabbed a honey bun from the display case when she wasn't looking and walked out to the house to drop off my books before the evening of slave labor and dodging land mines began.

I found Daddy doing push-ups on the frayed living room

rug. Roy junior rode on his back, up and down as if he was on a bucking bronco. I stopped and watched them, remembering how Daddy used to bounce me around like that. I hadn't noticed before but the muscles in his arms had become massive. From working out in prison, I guessed.

"Whatcha doin'?" I asked.

Daddy pulled Roy junior up over his head and stood. There was a wild look in his eyes that alarmed me. He seemed a little too excited, and he smelled funny, as if he'd spilled cologne on himself. His eyes darted around the room to make sure no one was listening, which was weird since no one was there. "Can you keep a secret?" he asked me. His breath was hot and sticky and overpowering. It made me nervous.

Real nervous.

"I reckon." I knew from his tone that something was brewing and I didn't want to be part of it, but I didn't know what else to say.

"I got a job," he said, beaming.

"You got what?" I felt as if I was sinking.

"A job. Down at the lumberyard. I start in a few days, but don't tell your mama. I want it to be a surprise. I'm gonna help stock at night after the yard closes."

"But don't you *gotta* tell her? She'll expect you to sing at the café," I said.

"Forget the dang café, Kenny. This is a real job. Real

money. I gotta do something more with my life than just sit around thumping on a guitar, pretending to be a man when all I am is a fancy centerpiece."

"Ain't you gonna tell her at all?" It seemed pretty obvious to me that she'd notice he was gone, since her entire existence centered upon him singing.

"Not till after I start. I don't want to jinx it by telling her. You know how she is."

Yeah, I knew.

"You gotta promise you won't mention it until the night I start. Then you can explain how I got a job but I couldn't say anything 'cause I wanted it to be a surprise."

"When's your first night?" I asked.

"This Thursday."

Thursday was the evening *Austin City Limits* was coming. That was about as perfect as a disaster could get. Mama was making me promise not to tell Daddy about the TV show and Daddy was making me promise not to tell Mama he got a job.

"I promise," I lied, wondering why they felt they could confide in me when they couldn't confide in each other.

"Thanks, son." He tousled my hair like he used to do when I was little. It made me feel proud. I don't know why. It made me think about Grandpa Willson, my daddy's daddy. We all called him Lefty because he was missing the ring finger on his right hand. It got chopped off when he was in prison for hot-wiring cars. He used to fart around with me like that. Grandpa Willson would mess with my hair, then he'd put me in a headlock and tickle my ear, telling me he'd lost his finger in there, saying I stole it. Of course that was before he got accidentally run over and killed one night while trying to steal a pickup from the Chevy dealership over in Welfare. Maybe my daddy wasn't so bad. At least he wasn't stupid enough to get himself run over. And he'd got himself a job. Maybe I even felt a little proud of him.

"I don't know when I'll be done on Friday morning, so it would probably help your mama a lot if you could cover for me at the café," said Daddy. "I know you got that contest thing, but you're just an alternate, right?"

With that comment my feelings of pride turned to anger. I was "just an alternate." I wasn't even planning on going to the UIL competition, but I'd thought he was on my side. Now I saw he was only out for himself. But I didn't let my anger show. I wouldn't give him that satisfaction. "Sure Daddy. No problem. It's no big deal." *Because I don't intend on being in the county come Friday.* I would swallow my words for a little while longer, and then I'd be gone.

"Thanks a lot, Kenny," he said.

Daddy left to walk to the grocery store. Roy junior opened the pantry and started playing with all of the boxes that made shaking sounds. He held one box of macaroni and cheese in each hand, wiggled in his diaper, and sang, "Shake, shake, shake. Shake your booty."

I sat and stared at the blank piece of paper that was supposed to contain my poem, but all I could think about was what a mess I was in, trying to keep secrets from everybody. I wondered how I could ever tell Mama about Daddy's job without getting hit upside the head. And how could I tell Daddy about his big musical break without upsetting Mama?

Roy junior took a can of Crisco out of the pantry and shook it. I knew that vegetable lard wouldn't make a rattling sound, but I was surprised when something inside the can went *thud*.

I tried to take the shortening container from Roy junior. He clutched it to his chest. "Mine!"

"Let me see that." I wrestled it away from him and peeled back the lid. The inside of the can was shiny and clean. And there was a bottle hidden in there.

"Southern Comfort." I read the label out loud. It was a bottle of whiskey.

Mama walked in. "Kenny, I need you out in the café." She froze when she saw me holding the liquor.

"It ain't mine," I said, realizing how incriminating that must have sounded.

I felt her hand before I saw it. It came up quick and hit me so hard across the cheek that I fell back against the wall, hit my head, and dropped the liquor. I saw stars for a minute. Then out of the corner of my eye I saw Mama pick up the bottle.

Don't lose your cool. You'll be away from her in a couple of days. Just keep it together until then.

Roy junior took one look at Mama standing over me with that bottle and he scrambled into a cupboard to hide among the pots and pans.

"Did you bring this poison into our home?" She didn't wait for an answer. "You and those no-account friends of yours. Did they put you up to this?"

She looked at me with eyes so hot with hate and disgust it seemed that the hairs on my head were getting singed.

I knew instantly who the bottle belonged to. But for some strange reason I felt guilty. Maybe I was just feeling guilty in place of my daddy.

"Mama, don't." I started to cry, but I stopped myself. I wouldn't give her the satisfaction of seeing me blubber like a two-year-old. I can't say if I was more upset because my mama was screaming at me or because I knew my daddy was drinking again. I scooted back across the floor away from her.

"Do you have any idea what you've done?" I couldn't understand why Mama didn't even seem to consider that the liquor belonged to Daddy. *Was she really that blind?* But then I'd been blind, too. Hadn't I seen the signs? She needed to believe that Daddy was okay. I guess we both did.

I could feel the walls of the house shake as she screamed at me. The whole place was sucking me down. I had to fight against the feeling of drowning.

"It ain't mine," I whispered unconvincingly. I knew it was a waste of breath, but I felt I had to say something.

Whatever you do, don't let her see you cry. Swallow your words. Swallow your anger. Swallow your pride.

"Your daddy is on probation. If they find one drop of liquor in this house the authorities could haul him back to prison and throw away the key. Is that what you want, to send your daddy back to prison?"

That seemed highly unlikely, since Jake had already seen a broken liquor bottle in the café and had done nothing. But now wasn't the time to confront Mama about her proneness to exaggeration. The truth was, at that moment I wished Daddy were back in prison.

Just then Daddy walked in from outside, all smiles, carrying a sack of groceries. But he lost his grin the second he saw Mama holding that bottle of whiskey. A look of pure horror filled his eyes and he lost all his color. There was a strange new rage in Mama and I believe it scared him even more than it scared me.

"Who do you think you are?" she screamed at me. "You will not destroy everything I have worked for my whole life."

I scooted back away from her. I don't know where I thought I was going. Maybe into the cupboard to hide with Roy junior.

Stand up for me, Daddy, I wanted to shout, but the words stuck to the roof of my mouth and never made it past my lips. He just stood there, silent and frozen. I wondered how it was that Daddy could stand up to Todd Anderson and the men in prison and not be able to stand up to Mama.

Mama hurled the bottle across the room. It broke against the wall above my head. I felt a shower of whiskey and glass falling down on me. The liquor smelled sticky and sweet and made me want to puke.

I felt a sudden burning sensation across my cheek. I reached up to touch my face and when I pulled my fingers away they were covered in blood.

"Good Lord, Maggie." Daddy pushed past Mama and hurried to my side. He tore off a piece of his flannel shirt and put pressure against my cheek. The cloth was soft and Daddy's hand felt warm and reassuring. At that moment I wished more than anything that the bottle belonged to me and not my daddy. I guess somewhere in the back of my mind I was hoping Daddy would be okay, that he wouldn't turn back into a drunk. Now I knew he'd always be a drunk.

"I'm sorry, Mama," I said, not sure what I was sorry for.

"You will go straight to school and come straight home every day." She was verging on hysteria.

"Maggie, stop!" Daddy's voice was firm. I was glad at that moment that he was between her and me.

"I will be on your ass like glue, boy. You ain't ruining us."

Daddy turned redder in the face than Mama. He jumped to his feet and spun around to face her. He grabbed her by the shoulders. "Stop it!" he screamed.

Mama crumpled like a fold-up couch. She sobbed and buried her head in Daddy's shoulder. "Kenny can't ruin us. Not now. Not after all we worked for. Not when we're so close."

"Ain't nobody getting ruined, Maggie." Daddy patted her on the head and cradled her until she finally calmed down. She looked over his shoulder at me, sitting on the floor with blood running down my face and the piece of Daddy's shirt clutched in my hand.

"My God. What have I done?" She cried louder, her whole body shaking. "Kenny, baby, I'm sorry." She started toward me. I backed away.

Don't touch me, I wanted to scream. If she touched me I'd smack her. That knowledge terrified me, because I knew that if I laid a hand on her I'd never be any better than Buddy Blackwell.

Fortunately, Daddy stopped her. "There now, Maggie. You're upset. Go on back to the café while I tend to Kenny."

She wiped her eyes with her knuckles. "I don't know who I am anymore," she whispered.

That made two of us, because I sure as heck didn't know who she was. Or what she'd do minute to minute.

"Go on back to work. I'll be out to join you shortly," Daddy told her.

"Okay," she whimpered as her guilty eyes swept over me. Her hand lingered on his for a moment, then she walked out the door.

Daddy got some water and tended to my wound. "You got a nasty cut, son."

"Yes, sir," was all I could think to say.

"You could use a stitch or two. Let's see what I can do." As he went to get the first aid kit out of the bathroom, I heard Roy junior dislocating pots as he scrambled out of the cupboard. He came up and sat beside me wearing a soup pan on his head. He wrapped his arm around mine and sucked his thumb. I patted his shoulder. The kid was scared. I felt sorry for him. Soon I'd be in Dallas and the poor little guy would still have another fifteen years or more of dealing with Mama. I wanted to scoop him up and take him with me, but I knew that wasn't possible.

"I'd stay if I could," I whispered to him. I wondered if he'd hate me for running out on him the way I'd hated Daddy for getting thrown in prison.

Daddy came back and put some rubbing alcohol on the cut. It burned to high heaven. I gritted my teeth but I didn't say a word. Daddy put a piece of tape across the broken skin to hold it together so we wouldn't have to go to the hospital.

"You took the heat for me, son; I appreciate that. Not many grown men would have done what you did."

"Yes, sir." I wanted to tell him I didn't have much of a choice, but he made me feel proud in a pathetic sort of way, so I let it go.

"They say 'once a drunk, always a drunk,' but that ain't necessarily true," he tried to explain as he packed up the first aid kit. "I just need a little nip every now and then when I get bored or worried over stuff. It ain't like it was before. It ain't ever gonna be like that again. I swear, Kenny."

But I knew it already was *exactly* as it had been before. The skulking around. The lies.

"You seen me drunk? You seen me staggering around like a fool?"

"No sir," I said honestly, but I remembered the basketball game and how Daddy kept going to the food stand and how he had reeked of cologne and I wondered just how long he'd been sneaking drinks. I wondered what he told the folks at the AA meetings or if he just lied through his teeth to them as he had to us. Or maybe he wasn't going to AA on his trips to Boerne. Maybe he wasn't going to Boerne at all.

"That's because I can control it now." He was honestly trying to believe it himself, but I could see a desperate uncertainty in back of his eyes.

Daddy took the first aid kit to the bathroom, then he returned. "I got a job now. Things are gonna turn around for us. You'll see." He was standing in the doorway and he looked smaller to me just then, even though his shoulders were so broad. I saw how deep the creases around his eyes had become. He looked small and weak and afraid and sure and strong all wrapped up into one. At that moment I loved him and hated him more than I ever had because I knew he was going down and I had a feeling that this time he wouldn't be getting back up.

I jumped up on my feet and stood looking him in the eye from across the room.

I wasn't going down with him.

Damn them all to hell. I wasn't going down.

Daddy scooped up Roy junior. "You rest, Kenny. Take the night off. I'll go help Mama."

He went out with Roy junior, leaving me alone in our tin can of a home. The wind picked up and I could hear it ripping through the cracks in the walls. I sat on the couch and stared at the blank piece of paper that was supposed to contain my poem. "Write about your environment," Mrs. Peterson had said.

My environment. That was a laugh. My sheet-metal-sided house, my drunk daddy, and my crazy mama. Those things didn't belong in a poem; they belonged in a joke book.

But the empty page kept staring at me, and I kept staring back at it until I couldn't stand it any longer. I grabbed a pen and started writing as fast as I could. Just trying to get words out of my brain, I guess.

I Ain't Going Down, Mama. I ain't going down. You can lock me up in your Coke can house 'til I'm busting at the seams. You can whoop me like a dog while I listen to your schemes. You can take

away my pride. You can pull me off the team. You can step on me
'til I squirt blood, but you ain't taking my dreams.

I kept writing until I'd filled up the page. Then I quit. I figured I'd go back later and take out the "ain'ts" and the improper language. But for now the poem was done.

I looked around to make sure I was completely alone, then I set down my pen, laid my head on the table, and cried.

chapter 15

After the incident with the whiskey bottle, Mama stuck to me like the star on the Texas state flag. She left Daddy to tend the café while she drove me to school. She wouldn't let me out of the truck until the bell rang. Then she'd be waiting at the curb as soon as I got out of my last-period class.

That's how I ended up accompanying her to Smitty's Liquors that following Tuesday. She told Daddy that she and I were going to the grocery store. It was no picnic keeping track of all the lies they told each other.

I was plenty irritated. For one thing, I didn't much like the idea of being in the establishment my daddy had robbed. For another, the note I had sent to Cindy by way of her sister Suzie had asked her to meet me out behind the café that afternoon so I could talk to her. There was a brief period each day when Mama let me go unattended to the dumpster to take out the trash. That would be long enough to tell Cindy the Plan. In my note I told Cindy to meet me at five. It was now four-thirty.

What we were doing at the liquor store I didn't know, but as soon as Smitty saw Mama he stiffened his back and his short fat neck turned rock hard. He took the rag he was using to wipe down the counter and mopped the sweat off his face. Smitty weighed about three hundred pounds and was an excellent candidate for a heart attack. He looked at Mama as if she was about to induce one.

"Hello, Smitty," said Mama sweetly.

"Maggie." He didn't look happy to see her.

"It's been awhile," said Mama.

"Can I get you something?" He went back to wiping the counter, avoiding her eyes.

"I came to ask you for a favor. Roy wants to talk to you."

More lies. All part of Mama's plan to make Daddy a "good" alcoholic. Daddy was as terrified of Smitty as Smitty was of him. I'd seen Daddy standing out in front of the liquor store, unable to go in. Wasn't that a joke? Obviously he'd found a liquor store somewhere he wasn't too nervous to enter and buy a bottle of Southern Comfort.

"If you could just come by the café . . ."

Smitty slammed his fist on the glass countertop before Mama could finish. "Maggie, you're a good woman. I got no quarrel with you. Let's keep it that way."

"Roy's doing real good. He quit drinking and I know his singing is gonna take off any day."

"All I *know* is that the man held a gun to my head." Smitty reached down behind the cabinet and took out a prescription bottle and emptied a pill into his shaking hand. He swallowed it without any water and tossed the brown bottle back behind the counter. I wondered if it was one of those nitroglycerin things doctors give you to take when you feel as if you're going into cardiac arrest.

"He was crazy drunk that night, Smitty. He's changed." She sounded as if she was trying to convince herself as much as him.

Daddy hasn't changed, I wanted to holler, but I wasn't going to be the one to educate her on the subject. So I just stood there staring stupidly at the liquor display.

Smitty glared at me in disgust. Maybe I looked a little too much like my daddy. I don't know. His eyes made me nervous.

"Mama, we gotta get back," I said, but she ignored me.

"Roy emptied my cash register. Took every dime." Smitty's face turned beet red and the veins in his neck were popping out. I wondered if Mama could be charged with murder if she gave the poor man a coronary.

"He took three hundred dollars and it cost him three years of hard time. He paid for what he did," said Mama.

Smitty hurled the rag across the room in anger, causing Mama to flinch. "He didn't pay his debt to me. You don't know what he took from me. You got no idea," he said, his voice low. Smitty stepped back away from Mama and as he did he bumped into a display case of Jack Daniels. The liquor came crashing down onto the floor. The old man crouched down on the brown linoleum while he picked up the fragments of glass, his hands shaking. "You two best be on your way." There was such strained control in his voice, I feared he would explode at any minute.

Mama knelt down beside him and gently touched his hand.

Let it be, Mama.

"Roy knows what he did to you was wrong," she told him. "He wants to make amends. It would mean a lot to me if you would come by the café. Let Roy get some things off his chest. Pay back what he owes you. He feels real bad about what happened. You know that gun wasn't loaded."

"When you're staring into the barrel of a forty-four you don't think to ask if it's loaded." I could see the terror in the man's eyes. I guess Mama could see it too, because she stood up and backed away.

"I'm sorry, Smitty. We're all sorry about what happened."

"I was a wreck. Did you know I lost my wife? I nearly lost my business, too. I was too dang scared to come back to work. I still can't even open the doors unless I got that rifle behind the register." Mama and I both looked over to see a rifle lying on a low shelf just under the counter.

He looked at the gun. Then he looked at me as if I was the one who had robbed him.

"Mama, let's get outta here," I said. I'd never had a person look at me with such contempt.

"I ain't a violent man, Maggie. But I know how to use that piece."

"Mama."

"I'm so sorry, Smitty." She didn't seem to know what to do. Whether to leave him alone in his misery or try to console him. She fidgeted with her hands as if she was trying to find a place to rest them. I figured the man probably didn't want any words of comfort from the person who had reminded him of his pain. Besides, he was looking at me weird again.

"Mama, let's go."

"You tell Roy I got a piece and I know how to use it."

"If there's anything we can do . . ." Mama touched his hand gently and he jerked it back as if he'd been bit.

"Mama, let's *go*." I pulled her by the arm toward the front door.

"You tell Roy that if he ever steps foot in here again I'll shoot him like a dog," Smitty yelled after us. Then he crumpled into a heap on the floor and sobbed.

"Good Lord, Smitty." Mama turned at the door and started back toward him.

I pulled her back. "Let him be, Mama," I said softly. "The man's already suffered enough over us."

She looked me over as if considering that I might actually have something of value to say. Smitty looked at me that way too. Mama nodded her head in agreement and we left.

We got out to the pickup and Mama handed me the keys. "You drive."

I slid into the driver's seat while she climbed in next to me. I was starting to feel like the family chauffeur. She put her face in her hands and cried. "I just wanted to make it right."

I wasn't sure what she had hoped to accomplish by the encounter with Smitty. I realized then that Mama had no understanding of the effect her actions had on people. Not on me or Daddy or the man Daddy had threatened with a gun. I wondered just how close Daddy might have come to killing Smitty that night. As crazy drunk as he was, did he know the gun wasn't loaded, as Mama had said, or was he just too drunk to remember the bullets?

Was Mama trying to help Daddy work his AA program? He obviously wasn't doing a bang-up job on his own. Was she trying to put right something she should have seen to long ago? Or was she simply trying to reassure herself that Smitty wasn't selling Daddy liquor?

In her mind I guess she only wanted to do what was right, but she wasn't really thinking of what was right for Smitty.

When I pulled up in front of the café it was ten after five. I got out and ran inside.

"Where do you think you're going?" Mama called after me. She had dried her eyes and was back to her old, ornery self.

"To take out the trash," I called back over my shoulder, heading into the kitchen before she could say anything else about it.

If Cindy were gone, I'd be mighty pissed at Mama. Of course, I didn't know for sure that Cindy would actually be there in the first place. She'd have to slip away from Todd. If she wasn't out by the dumpster I wouldn't know if it was because of Todd or because she didn't want to come or because Mama had been busy working Daddy's Alcoholics Anonymous program for him and had made me late.

I grabbed a garbage bag and went out back. But instead of Cindy, I found Suzie sitting there slumped over on a milk crate, looking awkward in a flowered dress, panty hose, and high heels. She looked up when I came through the door and I noticed she was wearing a wilted carnation corsage. She looked as if she'd been crying.

"Where's Cindy?" I asked.

"She isn't coming." Suzie took an already used Kleenex out of her white vinyl purse and blew her nose.

"Why not? Did you give her my note?"

Suzie stiffened at the accusation. She tried to stand, but she was a little wobbly. A bottle of peppermint schnapps fell out of her purse and landed on the blacktop.

I grabbed it up, grateful that it hadn't broken. The last thing I needed was for Mama to find a shattered liquor bottle out behind the café. I'd had about all the broken bottles I could tolerate in a forty-eight-hour period.

"You're drunk," I said.

"I feel like I'm gonna puke." She leaned on me.

"Well, don't puke here." I opened the trash sack to put the bottle of schnapps inside. As I did the lid came off and some poured out on my hand.

"Great," I said. "Now I smell like a peppermint girly drink." If Mama detected liquor on me, I'd be dead, and if I wasn't back inside the café in about two minutes I'd be whooped. I didn't know what to do so I reached my hand inside the bag and rubbed some garbage on it to cover up the smell. Old Frito pie, from the looks of it. Suzie looked at me in disgust. Then she puffed out her cheeks and got that look you get right before you're going to vomit, and she bent over and puked on my shoe.

"Good Lord, Suzie, how drunk are you?" I said, kicking off my sneaker.

She straightened up, took the used Kleenex back out of her purse, and wiped her chin. "I'm not so drunk that I'd wipe garbage on myself."

"Come on." I grabbed her arm and led her out toward the trash bins. The last thing I wanted was to have Mama catch me out back with an inebriated, puking girl.

I opened the heavy metal lid and threw the trash bags inside.

"Kenny!" Mama called.

"Dang!" I shoved Suzie behind the dumpster, then turned back toward the café. "Be right there, Mama."

"Hurry up!" she hollered. "We got customers." The door creaked as she went back inside.

I looked behind the dumpster where I had shoved Suzie and saw her sitting there crying, with her feet up in the air. "I'm sorry," I said. "I didn't mean to hurt you but I'll have heck to pay if my mama catches you out here." I reached out to offer her a hand. She slapped it.

She worked her way out of the crack between the dumpster and the retaining wall and brushed off her now soiled dress. "I'm not crying because you hurt me and I'm not puking because I'm drunk."

"Good Lord, are you pregnant, too!?" I blurted out without thinking.

"I'm not stupid enough to get pregnant. And I'm sure not stupid enough to marry that no-account pig. He's just like our daddy. I told her so. Anyway, how did you know she was pregnant?" She looked at me suspiciously.

My mind swirled in downward spirals. "Who got married? What no-account pig?"

"Cindy married Todd Anderson, you horse's spleen. That's why she's not coming. It happened at three forty-five this afternoon, in a brief and pathetic ceremony at the justice of the peace over in Boerne. And yes, I gave her your note. She told me to let you know she wouldn't be here."

"No, that can't be right."

"I was there. Believe me, it isn't right, but it's true."

I slid down into a heap and banged my head against my

knees. I felt as if someone had pulled the pavement right out from under me.

"She told me she had to marry him because she was pregnant. I told *her* I thought having one helpless dependent child would be hard enough. She didn't need two of them."

"I thought she was getting an abortion." My tongue felt as if it was sticking to the roof of my mouth again.

"That's crazy. She'd never do that. We're Catholic." Her eyes narrowed and she looked at me as if I was some type of conspirator. "Who told you she was gonna have an abortion?"

"I don't know, I just heard it around." I was thinking about Todd and my three hundred dollars.

"Kenny," Mama screamed. "Get your butt in here right now."

"I told you I'd be there in a minute," I screamed back at her, not caring anymore what she might do to me.

I heard the back door slam.

I stood up and walked toward the café without saying goodbye to Suzie. I felt as if I was floating, as if I had no legs, just rubber where my bones should be—a Gumby. I dreaded facing Mama, but I knew I had to. I remembered that I smelled like somebody's old Frito pie. I was wearing garbage, and I'd just yelled at her. Then I thought about how I'd given away three hundred dollars to a *pig* for an imaginary operation. Briefly I felt relieved that Cindy hadn't had an abortion, but the feeling was quickly replaced by the thought of wanting to kill Todd Anderson.

I tried to remember the exact procedure for choking someone to death by crushing their windpipe. Then I got disgusted with myself for having the idea.

I thought about the fact that Cindy was never going to Dallas with me.

And Dallas suddenly felt like a lonely, empty place even though I knew it was one of the biggest cities in the biggest state in the continental USA. Even though Grandpa Harris was there.

"What took you so long?" asked Mama when I came through the door. She sounded as if she'd just caught me holding up an armored car.

"Bag broke." I showed her my hand, covered in sticky cheese and cold chili.

She heaved her chest and shook her head in irritation. "Go get cleaned up. There's a party come in." I washed my hands at the sink as slowly as I could manage. Then I went out front. I saw the "party" and froze. Todd, Cindy, and Mr. and Mrs. Blackwell were squeezed into a booth. A little white bakery cake sat between them, the plastic bride and groom flattened facedown on the icing. In fact the whole cake looked as if it was about to fall over, as if someone had dropped it or something. Besides the "party," there were three truckers sitting at the counter. Jake was showing

Daddy his new police radio while Daddy warmed up for his evening of entertainment and lies.

I felt as if I was stuck in an episode of *The X-Files*.

"Go take 'em their drinks." Mama shoved a tray at me and pointed to the wedding group. They were all wearing grim expressions and wilted corsages.

"Mama, I can't."

"Of course you can. Just walk over there and give 'em their drinks." She looked down at my feet. "Good Lord, Kenny, where's your shoe?"

I looked down and vaguely remembered the vomit-filled sneaker out back. "It got garbage on it."

Mama's eyes narrowed. She grabbed me by the ear and pulled my face close to hers, smelling my breath. "Have you been drinking?"

"I ain't the drunk in the family, Mama," I said, not caring anymore how she might react.

She took a step back as if she'd been hit. She wanted to wallop me. I could see it in her eyes. But she didn't dare with a café full of people.

I turned and took the drinks over to Cindy and Todd and her parents. Cindy looked up at me with empty eyes. It was the first time in my life that I recall she didn't look pretty. It was as if every lovely thing had been sucked out of her. I wondered where it had all gone. I wished I could find it and give it back to her.

Mrs. Blackwell handed me a little box camera. One of those disposable ones you get at the grocery. "Would you take our picture? We seem to have lost our photographer."

I stared at them through the lens. "Smile," I said unenthusiastically. Mrs. Blackwell alone managed a forced grin. She'd overdone the makeup and neglected the black roots in her neat blonde hair.

I snapped the picture and handed her the camera back without looking at Cindy.

Won't that be a gem for the family photo album?

Then I walked back behind the counter and kicked off my one good shoe. I went around in my socks the rest of the night, hoping Mama would fire me.

Cindy ordered a cheeseburger. Todd and Mr. Blackwell had a Frito pie, and Mrs. Blackwell ordered a salad that, once it arrived, rivaled her wilted carnation.

None of them ate their food. They poked around at it without talking. I tried to avoid them, which wasn't difficult, because Mama, still angry with me, had me clean the bathrooms every time somebody went in to pee.

Suzie walked in about the time a cold crust was forming over the chili pies. She marched over and handed me my sneaker. I guess she'd been out back running it under the hose, because it was wet and clean. "Sorry about your shoe," she said. I could see she was as distraught over the recent nuptials as I was. I knew she idolized Cindy. I guess it was a blow to have her big sister go off and marry a scumbag. It made me think about all the things Cindy had wanted to be. All the dreams she had that she'd never realize. I couldn't look at her. I stared at my socks every time I had to pass her booth.

Suzie pulled a chair over from a table and plopped down with the wedding party looking as if she were a sixth finger, an appendage that didn't fit.

Buddy Blackwell instantly sprang to life, turning on his youngest daughter as if she was the cause of the evening's disaster and everyone's unhappiness. "Where have you been?"

"Out back puking."

Buddy grabbed the sleeve of her dress. "Don't be smart with me, young lady."

"Being smart doesn't seem to be a prerequisite for joining this family." Suzie looked across the table at Cindy and Todd. Todd looked at her blankly. Cindy stared at her hamburger.

Buddy squeezed the sleeve of her dress tighter. "How would you like me to drive you home, young lady, and pop you in the mouth?"

"Why, because your latest punching bag ran off and got married?"

Cindy touched the faded bruise around her eye.

Don't do this, Suzie. A feeling of dread for her swept over me.

I had been getting hints all night from Mama that I would pay for my comment about Daddy. Maybe she'd cool down enough not to hit me over it, but I knew there were a hundred ways to make a kid pay for a smart mouth. And I knew Buddy Blackwell would make Suzie pay for hers.

"Kenny, the bathroom trash needs to be emptied," Mama called as a trucker walked out of the men's room.

"Get up," said Buddy, lifting Suzie by the sleeve. "You're going home."

Just go, Suzie. Don't make him madder than he already is.

I realized then what a small man Buddy Blackwell was. When he stood he was barely taller than Suzie was sitting in her chair. But he was brawny and solid and mean. His shirt-sleeves were rolled up and tufts of reddish blonde hair covered a USMC tattoo on his bulky, muscular forearm. Those muscles flinched as he tightened his grip on Suzie's sleeve.

"No," said Suzie, wrapping her ankles around the legs of the chair.

"Get up, I said." Buddy tugged on her sleeve and dragged Suzie, chair and all, about three feet across the floor.

Poor Suzie. All she'd done to set him off was walk into the café. I understood well how a kid's mere existence could induce a parent to rage.

"Take your hand off of me," Suzie said through clenched teeth.

"Are you trying to tell me what to do?" Buddy turned red in the face.

"Suzie, honey, don't you think you should go on home?" said Mrs. Blackwell nervously.

Yeah, go home. Maybe he'll get drunk and forget he's mad at you. I felt sick for Suzie, as if I was the one Mr. Blackwell was picking a fight with.

"Kenny, I told you to take care of the bathroom trash," said Mama, coming up beside me. She stopped when she saw Mr. Blackwell dragging Suzie across the floor in the chair. Everyone was watching. I knew he was crazy. I just hoped he wasn't crazy enough to kill her.

Jake watched, keeping his distance. Jake followed the philosophy that family disputes should be handled within the family whenever possible. "Families should work out their own problems," I'd heard him say.

But when Buddy balled his meat loaf hand into a fist, Jake finally lumbered out of his seat and walked over. "You got a problem, Buddy?"

"Nothing a father can't handle."

"According to state law, I can file assault charges against you just for touching me," said Suzie.

Buddy looked at Jake standing there with the handcuffs dangling from his belt and immediately let go of Suzie's sleeve.

I didn't know if that was true or not, but it sure sounded good. I looked at Mama and smiled. She turned pale and looked away.

"There ain't no call to start threatening your daddy." Mr. Blackwell smiled nervously.

"I'm not threatening you, 'Daddy,' I'm telling you straight out how it's gonna be. You so much as touch me and I won't waste my time crying to a bunch of truckers and waitresses. I'll go straight to the law."

Buddy's neck stiffened. His eyes said, *You'll get it later.*

"I know what you're thinking," continued Suzie. "You think the law won't do anything." She shot a disapproving look at Jake, who stared at his handcuffs. "Maybe they'll lock you up a day at the most. Maybe only for the afternoon. But this is the way I figure it. You get about two thousand dollars' commission for every sorry bag of moving parts that you sell off that junkyard you call a car lot. More if you can pitch a radio or an air conditioner or an antitheft device. So if you get dragged off to jail way over in Boerne for the afternoon, it doesn't cost me anything, but it costs you two grand at least. More if you're having one of those promotionals."

Buddy plopped into the booth and scratched his pink head in perplexity as if he'd just been run over by one of his own used cars. He looked at Jake. The salesman's eyes were asking, *Can she do that?*

Jake smiled. "Smart girl." Then he took a toothpick out of his pocket, stuck it in his mouth, and rejoined my daddy, leaving Suzie to fend for herself, which she seemed to be doing just fine.

Suzie stood up. She looked exhausted, like the winner of a lightweight boxing match. "I'm going home now." Then she turned to her older sister. "Why on earth did you do it, Cindy? You want to end up like Mama?" Then Suzie left while her mother and sister tried to hide the fact that they were crying.

I respected Suzie just then. She'd grown up and she'd straightened out more than her teeth. She'd straightened out her backbone, and it was solid as a rock. She'd stood up to her father without losing her cool.

Wow, I wished I could do that, but if I ever opened the door, I'd never get it shut again.

After Suzie had gone the conversation around the café slowly picked back up.

Mama handed me the mop. "You best get after those bathrooms."

I handed the mop back to her. "With all due respect, Mama, I got more important things to do." I wanted to march outside, as Suzie had, and I would in a few days. I'd march out and never return. But for tonight I went into the kitchen and cleaned the deep fryer. That had her twisted up inside for most of the night. She didn't know whether to be mad or grateful.

After 2:00 A.M. folks started trickling in from the bars, which always boosted Mama's spirits. When I'd finally finished scraping the old pieces of corn dog out of the vat Mama said, "Thanks," so quietly it only minimally qualified as speech. But it meant her mood had turned and I probably wouldn't get whooped after all.

"Mama," I said as she started to take an order of nachos out to a group of cowboys. "Daddy got a job at the lumber-yard. He starts Thursday night."

The trace of what could have been a smile if the night had gone well faded. Mama walked out silently and waited on the customers. I went out to the house and went to bed before anyone had the opportunity to decide that I was the cause of his or her misery.

chapter 16

Mama was on the phone early Wednesday morning. "Roy just has a little family business to tend to tomorrow night. It would make all the difference in the world if he could start on Friday instead." As I was packing my lunch for school I heard Mama trying to convince Hank Tribble down at the lumberyard to let Daddy start work a day late.

"But *you've* got to tell him," said Mama, "'cause it's kind of a surprise. So if you could just say something about not needing him until Friday I'd really appreciate it." Mama's schemes had become so convoluted that I wondered how she kept them straight. I didn't know why she didn't just come out and say, *Roy's gonna be the next Randy Travis, come hear him sing.* She'd been telling everybody else. Except Daddy, that is. It was less than thirty-six hours before Daddy was scheduled to perform on national TV and Mama still hadn't informed him.

"He'll just fret," she kept telling me.

I walked to school and tossed my books in my locker. When I turned around, Cindy was standing there. I felt as if someone had punched me in the gut. She was back to her regular pretty self and for a moment I wondered if the entire "marriage" had been a bad dream. Then I saw the thin piece of gold on her ring finger.

She smiled. "We found a little house over by the hardware store. Daddy's even gonna help pay for it until we graduate."

"That's nice," I lied.

"Todd got a job. He'll work weekends until we get out of school. Then he'll work full time and if he gets overtime he'll be making really good money."

Marriage had actually started to agree with her and that made me nauseous because if that was the case then I figured she had resigned herself and the Cindy I knew was gone. Or maybe I never knew Cindy at all.

"I'm happy for you," I said, wishing the bell would ring.

"We're moving in next week but before we do I have to paint and Mama just bought the sweetest Winnie-the-Pooh wallpaper for the baby's room."

All I wanted was to get away from her. "Look, Cindy, I really got to get to algebra."

"So I can't go to the UIL competition this weekend."

Only then did I detect sadness in her eyes. She had traded all of her dreams for Winnie-the-Pooh and a house next to the hardware store. I wondered what would happen to the girl who sneaked out in the middle of the night to go hear poetry slams at coffeehouses.

"Oh Cindy —" I started to say, but she interrupted me.

"No, it's okay." She wiped away a tear. "There's not much point in me going now anyway. It would just depress me if I got a scholarship. But you can go. If I'm not there you can go in my place. You wouldn't be an alternate. You could compete."

A momentary flash of hope sparked inside of me. Cindy had won first place for the poetry competition and I'd won fourth. The only way I could actually compete was if one of the other students who placed couldn't make it. Now she wasn't going and I could take her spot. But that wasn't the way it was supposed to happen. Cindy wouldn't be there and if I won a scholarship, what good would it do? I wasn't graduating. You need a diploma to get into college. "I can't go," I told Cindy.

"But you have to," said Cindy.

"Mama won't let me. Besides, I got stuff to do." I closed my locker and started to walk away.

"Please," she said.

I turned back around. There was another tear in her eye. "Please do it for me."

"Honey, there you are." Todd walked up from behind Cindy and draped his arm around her as if to say, *This is my property.*

"Hi, honey." She mustered a smile. I could see they were both trying to sound married without knowing how. "I gotta go to physics. See you at lunch." She kissed his cheek and walked on down the hall.

The bell rang. I started to walk past Todd. He blocked my way. "About the money —"

"Forget about it," I said.

"She wouldn't have the abortion. But hey, it's okay. I kinda like being married. She's great. The best."

"Yeah, she is the best." I said. I knew it was true, but he sounded as if he had to convince himself.

"So I used the money to buy her a ring. But I'm gonna pay you back. I got a job at the lumberyard." His comment made me sick to my stomach. He'd used my money to keep Cindy and me apart forever.

"I gotta go to class." I pushed past him and hurried to math.

The day passed slowly. I entertained myself by counting the hours and minutes until I'd take the money from the café and catch the bus to Dallas. I fell asleep in computer class and dreamed about getting on a Greyhound. Cindy waved at me from the back, but when I went to sit with her, she had disappeared. I woke up when Francesca poked me in the ribs. The bell had rung and I'd slept right through it.

The Plan used to be about getting away with Cindy. Now it was about getting away from Cindy. And everything else.

I almost convinced myself to skip English. There was no

real point in being there. I was planning on dropping out of school in a day. But school was what felt like home to me and I thought I'd try to appreciate it while it lasted.

Besides, I'd been casually checking out Suzie since the incident at the café, to make sure that her daddy hadn't bruised her. I was worried sick about her, but so far she'd been okay.

Near the end of class, Mrs. Peterson walked over and stood in front of the blackboard. She was holding a stack of papers in her hand—the class poems.

"I can't say I was inspired by these; however, most of you made a good first effort at writing a poem. There is one, though, that stands out and I'd like for you all to hear it. It's titled 'I Ain't Goin' Down.'"

My blood froze in my veins. I hadn't had time to proofread the poem, or correct the grammar or the spelling. She was going to give everybody an example of uninspired writing, and the example was mine.

As she read the words I sank lower in my seat.

> *I ain't goin' down, Mama.*
> *I ain't goin' down.*
> *You can lock me up in your Coke can house,*
> *'Til I'm busting at the seams.*
> *You can whoop me like a dog*
> *While I listen to your schemes.*
> *You can take away my pride.*

You can pull me off the team.
You can step on me 'til I squirt blood,
But you ain't taking my dreams.

The class giggled when Mrs. Peterson read the part about the squirting blood. All except Suzie, that is. She shot me a look I couldn't quite read. I sunk even lower into my chair. Mrs. Peterson gave the kids a stare that could have frozen Dante's Inferno and they got quiet real quick. She was upset by the poem, that was obvious, and it wasn't any joking matter to her. She continued:

I ain't goin' down, Mama.
I ain't goin' down.
You can cook me in a vat of grease
You can drag me through the town.
I can't do nothin' to appease.
You still think I'm lowdown.
If it helps your troubled mind to ease,
Then I will be your clown.
But your Jack shack flack can't hold me back.
Though you pin me to the rack.
For one day soon, I will rise.
I'll mobilize before your eyes.
Your schemes and extremes I'll neutralize
'Cause I ain't goin' down, Mama.
I ain't goin' down.

She folded the poem into a square without looking up. Then Mrs. Peterson sat down at her desk and rested her face on her hands. She was crying.

I wanted to crawl under my desk and die. Mrs. Peterson was the most decent person I knew. I'd never do anything to intentionally upset her. That was the price for letting myself get so angry and writing that dang poem. I'd let down the one person whose opinion of me really mattered.

"Class dismissed," she said, still not looking at anybody. Everybody left but me. Suzie lingered for a moment as if she wanted to say something. I hoped she wouldn't so I avoided looking at her. She finally followed the rest of the class out.

I wanted to speak to Mrs. Peterson, but I didn't know what to say, so I just sat there. The clock hand ticked on slowly. She'd let everyone go ten minutes early. I kept thinking she'd say something, but she didn't. I thought about all the things I should apologize for. There were the obvious grammatical errors. The overall disrespect and I vaguely suspected that my rhyme scheme wasn't quite poetic. She looked up every now and then and started to say something, but then didn't. Finally, when the bell rang I walked over to her desk.

"I'm sorry" was all I could think to say. "I didn't mean to offend you."

"Kenny, is that what you think?" She reached out and softly touched my hand. "I read this poem because it was the best. I've read it to all of my classes today."

I couldn't believe what she was saying. "You gotta be kidding." I didn't quite understand. "What about all them 'ain'ts'?"

"Your poem was crude, I'll admit. But anybody can learn grammar. Anybody can learn to spell. That's the easy part. But nobody can teach you to speak from your heart. That comes from inside. Nobody can give that to you. You wrote from your heart, Kenny, and it moved me. You have a real talent and I hope you plan on pursuing it. Your grades are certainly good enough to get you into college, but it takes more than that. A lot more." Her voice trailed off sadly. I wondered if she was thinking about Cindy, her prized student, living next to the hardware store with King Kong and Pooh Bear.

"I'm not going to college," I told her.

She looked at me intently. "I can help you. There are scholarships and grants. It's not impossible for kids without money to get a higher education."

"It's impossible for me," I said, and I turned and left, sick about disappointing her. Not having any money for college was the least of my problems. You need a high school diploma to get into a university, and Mama would never let me get mine.

As I walked out the front doors of the school, Suzie stood up from the bench she'd been sitting on and walked over to me.

She stood in front of me and stared hard into my eyes. It

made me nervous for reasons I couldn't name. After what felt like an eternity she finally spoke. "Your words have power, Kenny. They can give people hope, and courage, and confidence. And they need that." Then she turned on her heel and hurried away before I had a chance to say anything.

I felt a surge of purpose. My words had power. If only I knew what to do with them.

When I got to the café, Mama was all abuzz. The excitement over all the plans had lit her up and made her look pretty, like she used to. I smiled to see her so happy but my own hopes were tinged with despair.

A deliveryman unloaded about three hundred boxes of frozen pizza while Mama tried to decide where to put it all. She finally resigned herself to the fact that there wasn't room in the freezer and threw out a bunch of old corn dogs to make space.

"Kenny, you gotta go over to the grocery and get some more plastic cups. And I want you to make name cards for all the important people and color code them, agents in blue and producers in yellow. That way when they see each other they'll know they've got competition. We might just get a bidding war started over your daddy. We've got so much to do. You're gonna have to stay home from school tomorrow and help me out."

"Okay," I muttered under my breath as I filled up the salt shakers in the kitchen. I didn't much want to face Cindy or Mrs. Peterson. I didn't like people being disappointed in me.

Mama emptied out the last of the honey buns and walked over to me. She smoothed my hair out of my eyes affectionately, then took both of my hands in hers.

"I know I been working you hard," she said.

"It's nothing," I replied, looking away.

"If I've driven you to drink, then I gotta take responsibility."

"Don't say that, Mama," I said in exasperation.

"I push you too hard. I only know two speeds—'high' and 'higher.'"

"You don't work me any harder than you work yourself, Mama." It was the truth.

"All the same, you gotta have a chance to be a kid. I'm real sorry about the way I acted the other day when I found that liquor. I was out of my mind." There was a tear in her eye. She wiped it away with the back of her hand, then hugged me, holding me close. She smelled like a combination of grease and lilac perfume and I thought the aroma was heavenly.

"It was nothing," I said, letting myself return the hug.

She let go of me and dried her eyes. "I'm gonna make it up to you, honey, I swear. Our luck is about to take a turn, you'll see."

She said it with such confidence that I almost believed

her. I suddenly wondered what would happen if she were right. What if we got rich and our luck turned around and our family got straightened out and I threw it all away to run off to Dallas? What if money actually did change things and Daddy was able to quit drinking and stay sober?

Just then we both heard a crash from the dining room. Mama and I both ran up front to see Daddy banging his guitar against the stereo where his voice singing "Comfort Café" was coming over the speakers. The tape skipped a beat but the music kept playing.

"How do you turn this crap off?" yelled Daddy.

Mama turned the stereo off, then grabbed his guitar and looked it over to make sure it was all right. "Roy, baby, what's wrong?"

Daddy, wearing a look of utter defeat, sunk into one of the restaurant chairs. "I lost the dang job."

"What are you talking about?" said Mama.

I figured this was liable to be an interesting conversation since nobody was supposed to know about the job.

"I got a job at the lumberyard. I wanted to surprise you, Maggie, make you proud. But Hank called me in today and told me he didn't need me after all."

"No, baby, I'm sure that ain't what he meant. Maybe he just wants you to start on another day. Maybe he wants you to start on Friday."

She hadn't acted surprised about the job. Daddy looked at Mama and me suspiciously. "Hank said he gave the job to somebody who needed it worse than I did. Some kid with a wife and a baby on the way, but I knew what he was really telling me. He didn't want *me* working for him."

I thought of Todd Anderson and got a sick feeling in the pit of my stomach.

"He gave the job away?" said Mama, looking guilty.

"Everything I ever touched has turned to crap. If you had a lick of sense you woulda left me a long time ago. Maybe you just get some kinda weird thrill outta being married to a loser." Daddy kicked over a speaker.

Mama quickly set it back up and checked the wire.

I wondered if Daddy was drunk. I remembered him running over my bike because it was in his way and I wondered what he'd do to Mama or me if we got in his way.

"Maybe you like being married to a bum." I'd never seen Daddy look at Mama with such hostility.

Mama walked over and put a hand on Daddy's shoulder. "Roy, baby, please don't talk like that. Another opportunity will come along sooner than you think. Wait and see."

"What other opportunity, Maggie? There ain't no jobs in this town unless they decide to let me run for sheriff and I don't see that happening any time soon. Ain't nobody gonna hire an ex-con."

Mama and Daddy both got real quiet. A heavy silence hung over the café. It seemed to me as if it was a good time for Mama to tell him about *Austin City Limits*.

"I've heard lots of people around town talking about

your singing. They love you, Roy. I expect we'll have a big crowd tomorrow night. Maybe it's just as well that job didn't work out."

Daddy glared at her and looked away.

She seemed to be thinking over how much to tell him. "I got a real good feeling about your singing, honey. I think if you just concentrated all your efforts on that—"

"When are you gonna get it through your thick head that I ain't a performer? How many ways do I gotta say it to you? I don't like to play the guitar. I don't like to sing and I don't like standing up here every night looking like a paid monkey on the end of a leash."

"You don't mean that, honey. Remember all our dreams."

"*Your* dreams, Maggie, and here's what I think of them."

Daddy picked up his guitar and broke the neck of it across his knee. Then he raised the splintered end, to throw it I guess, but it looked as if he was aiming it toward me. "When I was a child I spoke as a child, thought as a child, reasoned as a child; but when I became a man, I did away with childish things," I heard him say as I ducked down on the floor, covered my head, and waited for the blow.

But nothing happened.

When I looked up Daddy was laying the guitar neck on the table. There was a strange look in his eyes as he stared at me crouching down there on the floor. It was as if he'd looked into a mirror and seen a monster.

"Why are you cowering down there on the floor? Get up."

I didn't move.

"Get up, I said." Daddy strode over to me and lifted me up by my collar. Mama's eyes grew wide as she watched.

Hands still clutching my collar, he pulled my face close to his. His breath reeked of cologne. I guessed he'd been gargling with the stuff, to cover the smell of liquor. His eyes were wild and belligerent.

"Why were you cowering on the ground like a dog about to be kicked? I ever kicked you?"

"No, sir."

"I ever hit you?"

"No, sir." I could have pointed out the irony of his questions since he was currently strangling me, but I didn't think it wise to reason with a drunk. Sure, it was true he'd never hit me, but I never knew what he *might* do and that's what made me fear him.

"Then why are you acting like a dog?" He gave me a little shake.

That stung. He had no right to call me a dog.

I glared at him with all of the hatred I could muster. I could feel my body trembling. I remembered the UIL competition and how I'd stammered when I recited the poems. I would not let my voice reveal my fear. Not this time. Not ever again.

I made my words as cold as my heart felt at that moment.

"You're going down, Daddy. You and Mama both. But I ain't goin' down with you. Now . . . you . . . let . . . me . . . go!"

I did it. There was no fear. My anger had replaced it.

Daddy must have sensed something different in me, because he instantly let go of my collar and stared at his hands as if they were two evil agents.

Daddy grabbed his jacket and the truck keys off the counter and headed for the door.

Mama followed him in a panic. "Where you going, baby?"

"Why do you want to know? Don't you trust me?" Daddy hissed.

Mama looked away in guilt. She didn't trust him, but she didn't want to tell him to his face. That's one of the ironic things I've noticed about liars. They have a knack for making people feel bad for not believing in them.

Then, of course, there are those people who need to believe the lies.

"I'm gonna make myself into a man." Daddy walked out the door and jumped into the truck before Mama could tell me to chase after him.

chapter 17

Daddy didn't come home that night and Mama was in a state. People showed up all evening, asking where Daddy was and why he wasn't singing. Mama kept reassuring them that he'd be back and told them to be sure and return for the Big Night. The more nervous she got, the more she talked up Thursday. I finally went out to the house about three in the morning, but couldn't sleep. When I finally drifted off around four, I had a nightmare. I dreamed I was in the middle of a Stephen King movie and I couldn't get out. A possessed guitar and a wooden spatula were chasing me. The faster I ran, the faster they caught up to me. Then I heard the voice of Suzie Blackwell saying, "Relax, it's just a movie. It's got to end sooner or later." Then I woke up to the sound of Mama's frantic voice.

"Kenneeeey," she said as she hurried in from outside. She hadn't slept in three days and she looked it. She was running on pure adrenaline.

It was Thursday morning. The day of Daddy's performance. Mama plopped Roy junior down on top of me. "I got an errand to run. You gotta watch Roy junior and mind the café." She grabbed her purse and left.

I counted up the hours until the night would be over, I could take the money, and the horror show would finally end. It was seven o'clock in the morning. In twelve hours *Austin City Limits* would arrive and the crowd would start pouring in. They were due to start filming at eight. The show ran an hour. Then they'd have to pack up. I figured that was when I'd make my move. Mama would be all caught up in the festivities. I could take whatever money was in the cash register and leave. There was a bus departing the hardware store at 10:00 P.M. and I planned to be on it. Fifteen hours. I could hang on for another fifteen hours.

I'd had a total of about three hours of sleep. I splashed cold water on my face, then took Roy junior out to the café and fixed him a Pop-Tart sandwich. A trucker was up front banging on the bell. I wasn't in a hurry to wait on him and by the time I got to the counter he was plenty agitated.

It was a busy morning. I wondered if all Thursdays were like this. Truckers in every five minutes buying gas, sheep ranchers sitting around all morning wanting refills on coffee. I wondered where Mama had gone and how she'd gotten there since Daddy had the pickup. I had a sinking feeling that maybe she had to go bail him out of jail somewhere. Or maybe she'd run out on Roy junior and me and I was going to be left with a screaming kid and a restaurant full of folks expecting my daddy to sing.

Lunch came and went. We got about twenty people in and

all I had to serve them was partially thawed corn dogs, the ones Mama had thrown out the night before. That made everybody mad. Roy junior screamed that he was starving, so I stuck a chocolate doughnut in his mouth because by that time I'd run out of corn dogs. Fortunately he lay down and took a nap under the sink after that. Then, about one o'clock, I started to feel faint and realized I hadn't eaten breakfast or lunch or dinner the night before. So I defrosted one of the pizzas and ate the whole thing, even though Mama had threatened me with persecution if I touched them before nightfall. By then it was two o'clock. Just eight more hours until Blastoff.

But I couldn't go anywhere if Mama or Daddy didn't show back up to take care of Roy junior. Maybe they had met up outside of town and decided to ditch us kids.

Finally, about two-thirty, an eighteen-wheeler pulled up to the gas tanks and Mama jumped out, carrying a huge box inside the café. The box read, "Gibson's of San Antonio." Mama opened up the box and pulled out a brand-new flashy red steel-string guitar.

The trucker walked in. He was a big, burly man I'd never seen before. He handed me a credit card to pay for his gas.

"That's okay, Fred, it's on the house," she said to the trucker.

"That isn't necessary," said Fred. "It was on my way."

"Nonsense," said Mama. "Kenny, fill up Fred's thermos with coffee."

I took the metal thermos and filled it with Folgers. I could only guess that Mama had hitchhiked to San Antonio, bought Daddy a brand-new guitar, and hitchhiked back. A busy morning.

"Now remember," said Mama to Fred. "You be back here by seven o'clock tonight and you'll get all the free pizza you can eat."

"What did you say the guy's name was?" asked Fred.

"Roy Dan Willson. That's with two *L*s. And don't you forget that name because one of these days you're gonna see it in lights."

Fred left with his thermos, three honey buns, and a frozen pizza.

"You seen your daddy?" Mama asked nervously.

"Nope."

"That's okay. He'll be here," she said to reassure herself, I guessed, because she wasn't reassuring me.

The phone rang about three-thirty. Mama picked it up. "Yes, sir. We're all set up for tonight." I walked into the back and fell asleep next to Roy junior. Seven more hours. I woke up at four when Mama said, "Come on, Kenny, we gotta get ready for the show." She was out of her mind.

Still no Daddy.

I figured it didn't matter one way or the other now. We'd still get all those customers expecting to see him and they'd be eating pizza and drinking soda while they waited for "the next Randy Travis" to perform. They'd be filling up the register whether Daddy ever showed up or not. But if Daddy didn't show up, then I worried what would happen to Mama. Her entire world hinged on the events of that evening. I felt guilty for taking the money, but then I remembered that she'd worked me more than eighty hours during the last two weeks alone and she hadn't paid me a dime.

But what if Mama's world collapsed? What if she freaked out and ended up in a nuthouse? What would happen to Roy junior?

On the other hand, what could I do for the kid? No, I was better off just worrying about myself.

Four-thirty. Five and a half more hours until the bus left at ten.

At a quarter to five I walked up front, where Mama was busy sweeping the floor. "Start thawing out those pizzas," she told me. Just then the bells on the front door jangled. I looked up. Half of me was hoping to see my daddy. The other half was hoping to see anybody but him. It was Smitty walking in. He looked around nervously and stood there awkwardly in the middle of the room.

"I'm not sure why I came here," he finally said.

"Sit down, Smitty. Let me get you a cup of coffee." Mama pulled out a chair for him, then called out to me. "Kenny, get Smitty a cup of coffee."

The phone rang and Mama went to the back to answer

it. I carried the coffee over to Smitty. He picked it up and took a drink. His hands were shaking. He looked over the top of the cup at me, as if he was sizing me up.

"I owned that liquor store for twenty years without anybody ever trying to rob me. Never even had a shoplifter."

I looked toward the back, wishing Mama would return.

"My father owned the shop for fifteen years before that, and nobody ever tried to rob him. Before that my granddaddy owned a barbershop in the same spot. Nobody ever tried to rob him either. Not even during the Depression, when folks were starving. Then came your daddy." He took a sip of his coffee and watched me hard, as if waiting for me to respond. I looked away. Smitty continued. "He's the only criminal to speak of in this town. The only jail Comfort ever had was back in the nineteen thirties. Never got used. When the water district came in, they turned it into a pump house."

Mama walked back out front with a beaming smile on her face. She looked as if she was floating rather than walking. "That was Tri-Star Records." She sank into a seat next to Smitty but she was looking at me. "They said they couldn't get a representative out here tonight but they were definitely interested in Roy Dan Willson. They told me to tell him not to sign on with anybody else until they got a chance to make him an offer. Kenny, your daddy's gonna be big."

"What's going on?" asked Smitty in suspicion.

"Nashville is about to discover Roy," said Mama.

"How's that?" asked Smitty. "I thought he couldn't leave the county." The sarcasm in his voice was plain to me, but Mama didn't seem to notice it at all.

"They're coming here. *Austin City Limits*—agents, producers—tonight. Just to hear Roy sing."

"Roy's gonna be on TV?" Smitty's voice was cool. "Guess he got over that stage fright."

"He doesn't exactly know," I said, looking at Mama.

"He gets nervous. Better to let it be a surprise. It'll be okay," she said. "He's been singing for people every night. It'll just be a few more people than usual. He'll do okay as long as he doesn't have a chance to fret. The secret is not to let him stew over it."

"A lot more people," I said. "And TV cameras."

"It'll be okay. You'll see. Your daddy was born to sing."

Just then the bells on the front door jingled. We all looked up to see Daddy walking in wearing a day-old beard. Daddy and Smitty both stiffened noticeably when they saw each other.

Mama jumped out of her seat. "Roy!" Relief swept over her eyes as she ran up and hugged him as if he was a soldier returning from the war.

"I got a job," said Daddy. "In Welfare. At the grocery." He was beaming with pride and he looked tired, but he didn't look as if he'd been drinking.

"That's great, honey. Look who's here." She pointed to Smitty.

"I see him," muttered Daddy under his breath.

"It's okay," said Mama. "I told him you wanted to make amends. Remember the money."

She led Daddy over to the register and handed him the envelope. She'd been keeping it under the money tray.

Why hadn't I thought of that?

Daddy squared his shoulders as he faced Smitty. "I guess it's time to set this right," he said to her.

Mama motioned to me as Daddy sat down next to Smitty. I walked over to her.

"Let's give them some space," she told me.

"Mama," I whispered, "you gotta tell Daddy about tonight."

"I will," she promised. "As soon as he's done talking."

Mama went into the back while I swept the floor. Daddy pushed the envelope toward the large man sitting across from him. "That's your money, Smitty. It's all there. Every dime I stole from you."

Smitty opened the envelope, pulled out fifteen crisp twenty-dollar bills, and counted them nervously.

I sure could have used that money.

Smitty shoved the bills back into the envelope. "That isn't all you took from me. If that money had been sitting in a CD or a savings account these past three years it would've earned nearly fifty dollars. You gonna pay me my lost interest?"

Daddy looked at the register awkwardly.

"You got no idea the terror that goes through your mind when you're staring into the barrel end of a forty-four. It changes a man."

"Smitty, that night in the liquor store . . . I was scared too," said Daddy softly.

Smitty looked at Daddy in surprise. So did I. My daddy wasn't capable of killing anybody. I was ashamed for ever thinking he might be.

"Your life could be worse, Smitty. You could be me. It's one thing to have your nose in the barrel of a gun. It's another thing to have your finger on the trigger. I will *never* get over that, not in a million years. I will never forgive myself for what I done."

Smitty's hard scowl softened just a little. He studied Daddy as if he was trying to decide whether or not to keep hanging onto his grudge.

"Every time I hear the bells on the front door I break out in a cold sweat. I lost my family," said Smitty.

"I understand how you must feel," said Daddy, looking at the table in shame, unable to look the man across from him in the eye.

"I'm losing my dang hair," yelled Smitty, "while you're getting ready to go on national TV. So don't sit there and try to tell me how awful your life is compared to mine."

"What are you talking about?" asked Daddy. "I ain't going on TV."

Mama walked into the dining room and froze.

"Where have you been, Roy?" Smitty said. "Don't you have a clue what's going on right under your nose?"

"Maggie?" Daddy looked at Mama in suspicion.

"I was about to tell you," said Mama.

I guess Smitty decided to hang onto his grudge a while longer because he was suddenly on a roll and he seemed to want to ride it for all it was worth. "You're gonna be a one-man pony show tonight, Roy. Agents, record producers, TV cameras."

Daddy jumped out of his seat, his eyes dark. He looked like a caged animal. "What have you done, Maggie?"

"It was gonna be a surprise, honey."

Smitty snatched the envelope full of money from the table. "So don't try to tell me how sorry your life turned out, Roy, 'cause you aren't the one who has to keep a rifle behind your cash register just so you have the nerve to open the front doors of your store."

As Smitty walked out, Daddy winced, doubling over as if physically ill, grabbing the table for support. "What have you done, Maggie?" he whispered.

"I sent out a couple of tapes of you singing. That's all."

"Behind my back? Don't you remember what happened in Kerrville?"

"That was different. I was sick. You were still drinking then. It's not the same now that you're sober."

The uncertainty in Daddy's eyes turned to full panic.

I slipped into the kitchen, where I could hear them without being seen. Five o'clock. Five more hours. I just prayed that we all made it through the next five hours.

"Those folks in Nashville love you, Roy."

"They're coming here?"

"Just a couple of record producers and *Austin City Limits*," said Mama.

"A couple of record producers? What was going through your mind, Maggie?"

"Don't worry, Roy. They're gonna love you. They already love you."

"They ain't gonna love crap 'cause I ain't gonna sing."

"Roy!"

"I am *nobody*, Maggie. Why do you keep trying to make me over into something I ain't?"

Mama's voice got very soft and I had to strain to hear her. "I do love you for who you are, honey. But part of who you are is the best darn country-and-western singer I ever heard. I swear it. You got the talent, Roy. If you just had one ounce of self-confidence you could go all the way."

"You really believe that?"

"I do."

There was a long silence, then I heard Daddy speak. "Well, I don't."

Mama screamed, "No, Roy, don't."

I ran out into the dining room to see Daddy lift the shiny new guitar and smash it into pieces on the floor. Mama crumpled into a heap, picked up the pieces, and erupted in tears of despair. Daddy walked out toward the back. He glared at me when he saw me. "I guess you knew about this?"

"She made me promise not to tell," I said, recalling how I'd also promised not to tell Mama about Daddy's job, realizing there was no way to ever win in my family.

"Yeah, right," he said and went out to the house. I felt as if he'd punched me in the gut. I'd let him down. But there was no way to keep from letting him down.

Mama walked into the kitchen like a zombie. She came out with a huge box and put the pieces of the new guitar inside. "Kenny," she called out to me. "Get busy with those pizzas. We're expecting a crowd tonight."

Mama had obviously snapped.

Five-thirty. Four and a half more hours. I couldn't make it. Somebody was fixing to get hurt and I didn't want it to be me. I had to get out of there fast. We'd had a busy day. There was plenty of money in the register. I'd take what was there, add it to what I had in the box, and run. I could lay low until the bus came at ten, or I could hitchhike to San Antonio like Mama had done. Or maybe I'd hitchhike all the way to Dallas and save the bus fare. It didn't much matter to me at that point. I just knew that I couldn't stay in that café for one more second.

I kept my eye on Mama. She was crying and filling up the

box with pieces of guitar. I quietly opened the register, pulled out the stack of twenties, and slipped them into my pocket, leaving enough money for change so I wouldn't be discovered right away. Then I walked out to the house. Daddy was in the bedroom with the door shut. I quietly went into my room, slipped some clothes into my backpack, took the cash out of my pocket, and counted it—one hundred dollars. That would have to do. I reached under my bed for my money box.

It wasn't there.

Frantic, I lay down and swept my arm, as far as it would reach, across the floor. Nothing. I pulled off the mattress and box spring and threw them against the far wall. There was nothing under the bed but two pair of dirty socks and a chocolate candy wrapper.

My mind churned. *Who had taken my money?*

Was it Daddy? Todd Anderson?

I heard Roy junior singing in the living room, "Shake, shake, shake. Shake my booty." I raced out of my room to see him shaking my money box. The coins inside jangled as he giggled at the sound.

"Roy junior. That box is mine. Give it to me."

"No. Mine." He ran into the kitchen.

I chased him and tried to grab the box but he turned away from me so I couldn't get a good hold on it. "I'm not fooling. Give me that box," I yelled.

He ran back into the living room, taunting me to chase him. "Shake, shake, shake."

I grabbed the box and played tug-of-war until it broke open and money flew across the room.

Just then, Mama walked in with the box of guitar pieces. She looked at me, then she looked at the backpack, then at the money lying all over the floor. Then she looked past me into the bedroom at the money lying on my dresser.

She set down the guitar pieces. "Where do you think you're going?"

"No place."

She fell to her knees and quickly counted through the larger bills. "You got at least three hundred dollars here. I don't guess I need to ask where it came from."

"That's my money," I said through clenched teeth. "I earned every penny of it."

Daddy came out of the back room and gaped when he saw the money lying out on the floor.

"You steal from me, boy, and you got the nerve to tell me this is your money?" Mama yelled.

Daddy looked from the pile of money to the door as if calculating his escape.

"I've worked in that café like a dog and you haven't paid me one red cent. I'm going to Dallas and I don't care what you say. I'm gonna find Grandpa Harris and I'm gonna live with him. I'm sick and tired of Daddy. I'm sick of the café. I'm sick of this town and I'm sick of you."

Daddy looked away in shame. Mama stared at me coolly and didn't speak for what seemed like a full minute. Finally she said, "So you think you're gonna just run off and find Grandpa Harris and then your life is gonna be peachy."

"That's right."

"In Dallas?"

"That's right."

"Kenny, your grandpa, my daddy, was in Dallas five years ago. He's been in at least ten other towns since then."

"You're lying."

Rage burned in her eyes. She tightened her fists but she kept her voice steady. I'd never seen her so angry, yet so composed. "You're right. I'm lying. It's probably more like twenty towns, only I don't know them all because he only writes once every other year." She grabbed two postcards from the junk drawer in the kitchen and slapped them down on the coffee table. They bore postmarks from Tahoe and Tallahassee. I couldn't believe what I was seeing.

"My daddy wouldn't take no responsibility when I was a kid. He ran and hid like a coward in towns with fancy names while my mama worked herself into an early grave." Mama looked at Daddy, who hung his head. "I been trying to make your life different, Kenny, to make all our lives different. It would be nice to have a little help."

I couldn't listen. All that I could think about was that Grandpa Harris had sent us those postcards and that Mama had never told me. "Why didn't you call him or write him?" I said.

Mama's face turned three shades of red. She shoved the

postcards in my face. "Read 'em. There ain't no phone number. There ain't no return address."

I read them. She was right. But that wasn't the Grandpa Harris I remembered. *My* Grandpa Harris had told me to come visit him in Dallas, anytime. *My* Grandpa Harris was a rich worm farmer.

Mama looked from me to Daddy, disgusted with us both. "It's always what *you're* gonna get out of it, isn't it?" I wasn't sure to whom she was speaking. "Has anybody noticed that I don't sleep? Has anybody noticed I don't eat? Has anybody noticed that this is a family? That is supposed to imply that we pull together. I am sick and tired of carrying the burden around here. You are both pathetic. You are dead weight, and I'm tired of hauling you around."

I wished she would just hit me. It would have been better than standing there, feeling her words cut into me like daggers. Mama picked up the cardboard box filled with guitar pieces and threw it at Daddy's feet.

"Play tonight, Roy, or don't play. I truly do not care one way or the other. I've already got one record company that wants to sign you on. Believe me, you *will* sign and you *will* sing for their label and you *will* stop cowering around like a spineless animal. I've worked my butt off for the past three years to make something out of you, and not even *you* can ruin that."

She turned to me. "You." She shook her head, picked up

the money off the floor. Then she marched into my room and snatched the money from the dresser. "You'll find the register locked henceforth. On Monday we go down to that school and withdraw you. You're staying here where I can watch you every second of every hour of every day."

She left. Daddy and I stared at each other blankly.

It was six o'clock. The bus was leaving in four hours and I was going to be on it. I didn't know how, but I was getting out of town, or I was going to die trying.

chapter 18

I always wondered how a person decides to become a criminal. It wasn't exactly something you chose when career day came around at school. For me it happened that Thursday night when I simply figured out I could not bear my life for one more minute. Maybe that was how it had happened for Daddy three years ago. I suppose desperation led a lot of people to do a lot of things they'd never think themselves capable of otherwise. In a strange way I felt that I really understood Daddy for the first time. He must have had his reasons for doing what he did, just like I had mine.

My plan was to take off as soon as the TV cameras showed up at the café. Mama would be distracted. My backpack was still loaded with my belongings. I didn't have a ski mask and I thought that putting a pantyhose leg over my face was just a little too weird, so I found an old knit winter hat, pulled it down, and cut out eyes with a pair of scissors. Then I put the hat in the backpack. I didn't worry about a gun. I found an old stick that looked about the right size and put it in my pocket. I saw how scared Smitty had been with Daddy. I figured I'd work off the element of fear rather than the threat of a real weapon. Besides, if I got caught I couldn't be charged with armed robbery if I wasn't armed. I figured the worst that could happen to me was that I would be hauled off to some boys' prison. In truth, that would probably be a step up from where I was.

Even without Grandpa Harris at the other end of the line, I had to get out of that town. It wasn't so much anymore that I wanted to be somewhere else. I wanted to be *anywhere* else.

I planned on walking down the road and seeing what happened. There were plenty of potential establishments to plunder—the hardware store, the grocery, and the bookstore. The problem was that I knew all those proprietors and I didn't much feel like taking their money or giving them a fright, either one. In truth, there was a sick feeling growing in the pit of my stomach.

When Mama wasn't looking, I hid my backpack behind a potted plant near the front door.

I went back into the kitchen. Mama shoved a pizza at me. "Table four" was all she said. She didn't even look at me. If she thinks I'm scum then why not act like scum, I reasoned. I carried the pizza out into the dining room. Suzie Blackwell sat at table four along with Francesca Adams and her parents. Dr. Adams wore a crisp blue button-down shirt and loafers. Francesca had a suitcase next to her on the floor, packed and ready to go to Austin for the state championship, I figured.

"How you doing, Kenny?" said Dr. Adams.

"I'm okay, sir."

"It looks like you're expecting a crowd for the big night," said Mrs. Adams, looking around at the mass of people gathering in the café.

"Yes, ma'am."

"Mrs. Peterson wanted us to remind you that the bus leaves at seven-thirty tonight for Austin," said Suzie eagerly.

The UIL competition felt like a faraway dream. "I can't go," I said in a whisper, hanging my head low. I had tried to push the state championship out of my mind. I figured there was no use in hoping for things you can't have. But when I saw Francesca's suitcase, I was jealous.

Dr. Adams's eyes grew dark and serious. "Would you like me to speak with your mother, Kenny?"

I was taken aback. I couldn't see any reason why Dr. Adams should go out of his way for me. "Thank you sir, but no. To tell you the truth, poetry feels like a frivolous cogitation when the encumbrances of life imprison you." I don't know why those words popped out of my mouth, but as soon as they had, I felt as if I'd taken out my vocabulary and dusted it off.

Francesca and Suzie narrowed their eyes, trying to figure out what I had just said. Dr. Adams just smiled. "I believe Maya Angelou would disagree with you."

"What would Ms. Angelou say on the subject?"

"She'd say 'I know why the caged bird sings.'"

I remembered that Dr. Adams had been present at the district competition when I read the Maya Angelou poem "Caged Bird."

"I don't see what the caged bird has to sing about," I said, trying to hide my discomfort.

"Freedom. Those who are not free are the only ones who truly understand the word."

"I don't sing," I said with regret.

He nodded in understanding. "You're a good, decent boy, Kenny. If you ever need anything, let us know."

"Kenny, get in the kitchen," yelled Mama.

"Thank you," I said to Dr. Adams.

As I walked back toward the kitchen I spotted another guitar sitting up next to the stereo. It wasn't shiny or new. The varnish was peeling and the ends of the strings were frayed. I wondered where Mama found it. There weren't any pawnshops in town. Maybe she got it from the Comfort Emporium, or even one of the antique shops. It looked old enough to be an antique.

I delivered three more pizzas. Daddy walked in wearing the blue Elvis shirt and tried to kiss Mama on the cheek. She recoiled and kept wiping the counter without looking at him.

Daddy sat down at the counter. I could tell something was stirring in his brain. It worried me, but I had enough problems of my own to fret over. I couldn't borrow his. He reeked of cologne, which I had finally learned to associate with his covering up the smell of liquor. I wondered where he was getting it. He had the ability to be resourceful when it came to his addiction. Too bad he couldn't be resourceful any other time.

Daddy drank a soda. A few truckers came in, then a bunch of people from out of town. The place started to buzz with conversation. Daddy could barely hold his glass, his hands were shaking so. I seriously doubted if he could hold a guitar. I felt a wave of pity for him, remembering how I had felt standing up to recite poetry at the UIL for the first time. On the other hand, he also disgusted me.

There was something I had to ask him. "Daddy, did you ever kill anybody when you were in prison?"

He narrowed his eyes and took another drink of soda. "Do I look like I could kill somebody?"

"You didn't answer my question."

"There was this old guy about to make parole. The day before he was supposed to get out, he hung himself. I was the one who found him."

"That don't make no sense. Why would he kill himself if he was getting out?"

"Hell if I know," said Daddy, gulping the last of his soda.

He turned away from me, indicating that the conversation was over. Mama walked over and started filling a drink order.

"I'm gonna be sick," Daddy told her.

Mama didn't respond.

"Look at me, Maggie," he said to Mama.

Mama rearranged the chip display to avoid his eyes.

"Dang it, Maggie. Show me some respect."

No response.

"I'm going out for a while."

"You can't go now. *Austin City Limits* just got here," Mama said as a van pulled up outside and men with cameras started getting out.

"You think you can stop me?" asked Daddy. There was venom in his voice.

Mama's face hardened. "I'm telling you that if you step foot out that door now, you ain't ever coming back in. This is *my* night, Roy. Don't you dare try to mess it up."

Daddy stared at her in hatred and revelation. Even through his dazed eyes he could see what I saw. Everything Mama did, she did for herself. What disgusted me most was the way she tried to disguise it as virtue.

"I don't know who's crazier, Maggie, you or me," said Daddy. Then he stalked out the back door.

Mama's face turned from anger to panic. "Go after him, Kenny. You gotta stop him."

"No, Mama. You go stop him." I looked toward the front door and wondered if I could make it out before my mama could come around the counter to try and restrain me. I tore off my apron, threw it on the floor, and bolted for the front exit. I bent down to get my backpack, and when I stood up, Suzie was next to me.

"Whatever you're thinking of doing, Kenny . . ." She hesitated, looking from the backpack to my eyes. "Remember, there are people here who care about you."

I looked around at the people in the café. There were good, decent people like the Adamses and like Suzie. They were on my side. I knew there wouldn't be people like that where I was heading. I felt a lump of regret in my throat. Then I saw Mama grab a wooden spoon and start my way. I imagined what it would feel like hitting me across the face.

"I got no choice," I said and I ran out the door.

"Don't let them win," I heard Suzie say.

"Kenny," Mama yelled from the front door when I was halfway down the road. I kept running as fast as I could until her voice faded behind me into the wind.

That's the last time I'll hear her voice screaming at me. That's the last time I look into his lying eyes.

And that's the last time anyone will say they care about me.

chapter 19

I kept running and I didn't stop until I got out to Highway 27. I slowed down and started walking east. There was a gas station up the road about a mile ahead. Some folks new to town had bought the place. I didn't know them personally. That would make what I had to do easier. One day I'd have a job and I'd be making money. I could send them back whatever I took from them. I walked and walked. With each step I felt a knot growing in my stomach.

These are innocent people, I told myself. *Yet I got no other options.*

" 'The caged bird sings of freedom,' " a voice whispered to me. But what did "freedom" mean? I wasn't sure I knew.

There were two buses leaving that night—one for Dallas and one for Austin.

Two roads diverged in a yellow wood.

If I fled to Dallas I'd go as a criminal. If I went to Austin I might win the poetry competition, but I'd just be returning to Comfort to become a high school dropout.

Long I stood.

I doubted if I should ever come back.

My feet felt like lead weights. It took all the energy I had to put one in front of the other and move toward that gas station.

I finally made it to the Smokehaus Sausage Palace where I could smell German sausages sizzling on the stove and hear old Mr. Lowenstein playing his concertina for his customers. I went past the Comfort Emporium, where Mrs. Hodge kept vigil over her trash.

Then I came to Smitty's. I could imagine him wiping dust off the bottles and I thought about how lonely he was and how he'd lost his hair and his wife.

I couldn't bring myself to look. I hurried past so he wouldn't see me. I found myself standing in front of the filling station.

"This is it," I said, trying to give myself a little confidence, but it's impossible to ever feel confident about something that you know in your gut is wrong.

I thought about Roy junior growing up without anyone to teach him yes from no.

I looked back down the road at Smitty's and the Emporium and the Smokehaus Sausage Palace. I thought about the Adamses. I wondered what it would feel like to be a normal person in that town from a normal family. I realized for the first time that I didn't want to run from Comfort. What I wanted was to be a real and true part of it. But Mama would never let that happen. I was overcome with despair.

I didn't know what to do. I couldn't go forward and I couldn't go backward.

I felt the Black Pit beckoning me.

I felt the night coming to cover me.

There were poets in my head waging war for my soul.

I opened my backpack and started to pull out my hat. It wasn't there. I panicked and emptied the contents on the sidewalk. No hat.

I caught my reflection in the glass window of the filling station. I didn't recognize myself. I looked like a stranger, with dark, crazed eyes.

"What am I doing here?" I said out loud.

I looked inside and saw the clock. It was seven-twenty. In ten minutes Mrs. Peterson and the others would be leaving for Austin.

That was where I needed to be. I'd been heading for the wrong bus all along. It was time to change direction and get on the right one.

If I ran like the wind, maybe I could make it. I wasn't sure what I'd do when it was over. Mama was determined to keep me out of school. But I knew I had to go. I didn't know where that road would lead. I only knew I had to follow it.

I took off at a sprint in the direction of the school.

Everything would be okay, as long as I made it on that bus. I felt alive. I had real hope for maybe the first time in my life. The UIL wasn't a way to get money for leaving town. It was a way to stay and gain the confidence to endure whatever came. I knew my course, even if I didn't know where that course would take me. It gave me command of my destiny.

I ducked as I ran past Smitty's so he wouldn't see me. But when I got about five steps past the liquor store, I heard an explosion behind me. I got hit by a piece of flying glass and blood gushed out of my hand. A huge hole occupied the space where his big front window used to be. I looked inside to see Smitty holding his rifle. He had just blown out the front of the liquor store.

"Get out!" he screamed.

At first I thought he was talking to me. Then I saw the man standing across from Smitty. I couldn't really make him out but I could see that his face was covered and he was wearing a light blue shirt with what looked like a lot of fringe.

"Daddy!" I yelled.

Daddy stood there pointing a revolver straight at Smitty. His hand was shaking. He didn't seem to hear me. He wore my knit hat over his face. All I could see was his eyes. They looked scared, as if they belonged to a caged animal.

"All I want is enough money to get out of town," I heard Daddy say. "Then I'll leave you in peace."

"I'll leave you in pieces," yelled Smitty. He was beet red from his bulging face to his hands wrapped around the rifle.

I got a good look at Smitty. I didn't see fear behind his eyes. I saw power, fueled by rage. Fear is what I saw in my daddy's eyes. Not even the hat pulled down over his face could conceal that. But he still wasn't backing down.

Smitty pointed the rifle straight at Daddy's chest.

"No!" I screamed.

I heard the shot ring out. Then I saw Daddy fly backward into the display case, grab his chest, and double over.

I heard someone behind me say, "My God. Call an ambulance."

I kicked the glass out of the already broken window, hopped inside, ran to my daddy, and knelt down beside him.

Smitty. The power draining from his eyes was replaced with horror. He dropped the rifle on the floor and looked at it in disgust. Looked in revulsion at his hand that had pulled the trigger. Caught his reflection in the glass and looked away in shame. Saw me standing there and started to cry.

Daddy. Coughing up blood. Crumpled on the floor in a pool of red.

Jake. Pushing open the front door, shoving the display case out of the way. He pulled off the knit hat to reveal Daddy's face.

Jake ripped open the fancy blue stage shirt. There was a huge hole in Daddy's chest where the bullet hit.

"Get me some towels," Jake yelled at Smitty.

Smitty ran into the back.

"Dang, if I didn't make a mess out of everything again." Daddy tried to smile at me, but his smile collapsed into pain as he coughed up more blood.

"Don't say that," I told him. I tried to smooth the hair out of his eyes but I just got more blood on his face from the wound on my hand.

"Guess I won't be messing up your lives no more," he said. He coughed and more blood came out of his mouth.

I was crying, wondering why my daddy couldn't be normal, wondering why my family couldn't be normal. Wondering if there was any hope of me turning out normal. "You're gonna be all right, Daddy. Isn't he, Jake?"

"Yeah, sure he is," said Jake.

I wasn't just asking if he was going to live, I wanted to know if we were going to be *okay*. Would my family be all right? Then I cried all the harder because I knew the answer was no.

The clock on Smitty's wall read seven-forty. I'd missed the bus.

Smitty ran back into the room carrying one of those long white cloths that goes around a towel dispenser. It looked as if he'd ripped it out of its holder. He handed it to Jake, who wrapped it around Daddy's chest as tight as it would go. It didn't help. Blood kept gushing out through the towel, turning it red.

"Damn!" said Jake, pressing his hand into Daddy's wound, trying to stop the bleeding.

"I can't feel my feet," whispered Daddy.

"Somebody call the damn ambulance," hollered Jake.

"Lord, forgive me," said Smitty, looking at my Daddy.

"Daddy, you gotta hang on." I squeezed his hand, but he didn't squeeze back.

"I don't think I can, son."

Smitty started hyperventilating. "It was self-defense," Smitty yelled at Jake. "He had a gun."

"Shut up and call for help," Jake told him.

Smitty hurried to the phone, but his hands were shaking so badly he couldn't dial.

I figured that everyone associated with the volunteer fire department and EMS would be over at the café waiting for my daddy to sing. By the time they got to Smitty's, it was going to be too late.

"You gotta promise me two things," Daddy said to me. "You gotta swear that you don't turn out like me. Make something of your life. Don't run from it like a coward. Like me."

I swallowed hard. That was one big promise. "I swear it," I said.

The volunteer EMS pulled up, sirens blaring, despite my fears that they wouldn't get there in time. Two men and a woman got out: Frank Bergman, from the hardware store, his wife, Molly, and Tony Boswell, who owned a dude ranch outside of town. They looked odd, wearing their dress clothes and unloading a gurney.

"And you gotta promise to take care of your mama for me."

My stomach grew tense. There was no way I could make that promise in good faith, but I didn't feel inclined to lie to a dying man.

"I can't do that," I whispered.

"You've got to. You're all she's got now."

"Daddy, please don't ask me."

"Will you please shut up and stop carrying on like you're about to die," said Jake. "If you croak, Maggie can dang sure take care of herself. Don't put that off on the boy. But if you do croak, I'll kill you."

The EMS volunteers loaded Daddy into the ambulance and drove him toward San Antonio, to the nearest hospital, fifty miles away.

———

Later they told us that Daddy's heart stopped outside of Boerne, just a few miles down the interstate from Comfort. They tried CPR and when they got to the hospital the emergency room crew tried to resuscitate him for another twenty minutes.

The official time of death was 10:05, the very time I had planned to get on that bus for Dallas. Francesca and Mrs. Peterson were on a bus for Austin. I was sitting in the hospital waiting room with Mama and Jake. A pink-faced intern walked out and told us the news. Mama crumpled onto the floor and sobbed. So much for all her plans.

So much for all my plans.

Mama called Mrs. Adams to make sure Roy junior was okay. She'd taken him to her house for the night. Then Mama went in and sat with Daddy's body until midnight, when the people from the morgue finally showed up and took him away. She just sat there silently, holding his cold hand. Smoothing out his hair. Jake and I stood there watching her through the glass.

On the way home we drove in silence in Jake's patrol car. We were about five miles outside of Comfort when Mama finally spoke.

"Did he say anything?" she asked me.

"Who?" I asked. I hadn't really heard her. I'd been looking out my window at the darkness.

"Your daddy," she said. "Did he say anything about me before he died?"

"I don't recall," I lied. I didn't want her knowing Daddy wanted me to take care of her.

Mama cried.

We got to the café and Jake fixed a pot of coffee. The crowd had long since gone, but the place was a disaster. It looked like the morning after a New Year's Eve party. Cold pizza and half-drunk sodas littered the tables. A huge banner draped across the room read "Roy Dan Willson."

Mama shook her head and sobbed, "All our dreams . . ."

I started cleaning up the mess, not knowing what else to do with myself.

"It wasn't supposed to end like this," cried Mama.

But I knew better. It was Daddy's story, not Mama's. Just like the sad songs he always sang, it had to have a tragic ending. It was the only ending possible.

chapter 20

Early the next morning Mrs. Adams brought Roy junior back to the café. He hadn't slept a wink over at her house and she thought he might do better at home. She also brought a cherry pie. Later that morning Mrs. Lowenstein brought us a pound of sauerbraten from the Sausage Palace. Food kept arriving all morning. I don't know why people bring food when someone dies. I guess they just want to do something.

There are words under the food but no one speaks them.

After the third arrival of fried chicken, Mama got tired of it and locked the door. Then she hung up a sign that read, "Closed for funeral until further notice."

"Where's Daddy?" Roy junior asked me.

"He's dead," I said for the twentieth time.

"But he's singing," said Roy junior.

"That's the stereo."

> *There is pain in Comfort.*
> *There is Comfort in pain.*
> *But I find peace of mind at the Comfort Café.*

Misery's at my shoulder.
Sorrow's my next of kin,
But they've grown to be familiar,
So I think of them as friends.
Take me home to where I belong.
Take me home though the road is long.
I'll make a bed of roses.
Lay me down in the grass.
'Til I find myself in Comfort at last.

Mama played that song over and over. She wanted Daddy to be buried in his new blue shirt and she had spent the rest of the afternoon trying to wash out the blood, but there was still a huge stain covering the satin. Finally she bleached it, which took out the blood but turned the whole thing splotchy white. Then she replaced the buttons that had been torn off and patched the holes.

"Mama, when's Daddy coming home?" asked Roy junior.

"He's dead," said Mama, sewing the last button onto the shirt. "People don't come back when they're dead."

"Why not?"

Mama rubbed her chin in thought, then she took his little hand in hers. "It's like Daddy's gone to a real fancy prison. They have parties all the time and they even got room service. He's having a dandy time. The only problem is there ain't no chance for parole and he can't have visitors."

"Oh," said Roy junior in understanding. I didn't know if I approved of her metaphor but it worked. Roy junior didn't ask about Daddy anymore.

Jake stayed with us, but he and Roy junior fell asleep around four o'clock that afternoon after eating one of the chickens. Mama woke them up and sent them out back to the house.

Mama played Daddy's song another dozen times.

> *Misery's at my shoulder.*
> *Sorrow's my next of kin,*
> *But they've grown to be familiar,*
> *So I think of them as friends.*

Mama called a funeral home in Kerrville and made the arrangements. I went to the bathroom. When I came back I heard her on the phone. "'Roy Dan Willson.' That's with two *L*s. You be sure and get it right now. 'Loving husband and father.'" She took a deep breath. "'And the best damn country-and-western singer that ever lived.'"

She listened for a moment. "I don't care what you think is proper. I'm the one paying for the headstone." She slammed the receiver, laid down her head, and cried.

When we finished cleaning the café, it was well past dark. Then we cleaned it again. We sat in silence eating a platter of sandwiches for dinner, then we cleaned it a third time. I guess we were just looking for something to do so we didn't have to think about Daddy.

I felt a strange connection to Mama. It was as if we didn't want to leave each other, but we didn't want to talk either.

"The arrangements have all been made," she told me. "The café's gonna fall apart if we scrub it any harder. Roy junior and Jake are asleep." She paused as if thinking over her next few words. "I say we go to Smitty's."

"Mama, are you crazy?" I said. "It's ten o'clock at night."

"There's likely to be blood all over the place," she said matter-of-factly.

"There is," I told her.

"Who do you think is gonna clean it up?"

"I don't know," I said truthfully. "Don't they have people to do that?" I'd never considered whose job it might be to clean dead people's blood.

"There ain't nobody to clean it up but you and me. Not unless you think Smitty should do it?"

"No," I said. I figured Daddy had caused the man enough grief.

Mama grabbed a bucket, some bleach, and two scrub brushes.

"Mama, I can't do it."

She handed me the bottle of bleach. "Of course you can. You can do anything you set your mind to."

We walked silently through the dark down the highway

to Smitty's with nothing to light our way but moonlight. We could have driven, but neither of us mentioned it.

There was no traffic and no wind. Just a divine stillness. It was as if we were frozen in a magical moment that we didn't want to lose, which was weird, considering the circumstances.

Then I realized what it was. Mama and I were just "being." There was no expectation, no yelling, no put-downs.

No words. Just connection.

We found the front door to Smitty's unlocked. We could have gotten in anyway, because the plate glass windows were shot out. I figured that if we'd been in a larger town, San Antonio or even Boerne, there would have been yellow crime scene tape around the building. But we were in Comfort, so we walked right in.

Mama turned on the lights, then went to the back and filled up the bucket with water. Then she brought it up front and poured in some bleach. She put on a pair of gloves, got down on her hands and knees, and scrubbed the dried blood.

It occurred to me that this could be a good way to get shot, then I remembered how scared Smitty had looked with that rifle in his hand and I wondered if he'd ever be able to set foot in his store again.

Every time Mama rinsed her brush, the bucket of water turned a deeper shade of red. Then she'd hand me the bucket and I'd pour it out and fill it up with fresh water. That was as much as I could bring myself to do. I stood there watching Mama with admiration. It wasn't until that night that I had any notion of just how strong she truly was inside. She'd just had all her dreams blown away, her husband killed, and here she was, scrubbing up Daddy's blood, worrying over the man who'd shot him. She was the most surprising person I'd ever known. She cried and scrubbed and cursed Daddy, then she cried and scrubbed some more. After seven bucket loads of bleach and water she pronounced the floor "clean." She didn't cry for Daddy any more after that.

"That is the last mess of Roy's that I ever clean up," she said as we walked back to the café.

When we got back home Mama showered. Then I showered, wondering if I'd ever really feel clean again.

Then we just sat there in silence, drinking coffee. The song was long over, but it kept replaying in my brain:

> *Take me home to where I belong.*
> *Take me home though the road is long.*
> *I'll make a bed of roses.*
> *Lay me down in the grass.*
> *'Til I find myself in Comfort at last.*

"Mama," I asked softly, "do you think Daddy was trying to get himself sent back to prison?"

She thought about it as she sucked in a long sip of coffee. She looked at me thoughtfully and said, "I don't know, Kenny. He seemed to prefer that option to fortune and fame. I thought I understood your daddy. Now I realize I never did." Then her eyes became sadder than I'd ever seen them. She looked out the window into the distant night as if she were looking for a thing she knew she'd never find. "Sometimes a person just needs so desperately to believe in something." She set down her coffee cup and stood. "I've had enough. I'm going to bed."

I went to bed too, but I couldn't sleep. I felt something stirring inside of me. I recognized it as the old feeling that made me want to run, only now I knew it wasn't a place I was running from. It was something deep inside of me that kept calling me to be like my daddy. That's what I was trying to escape. The voices that sang out a song of misery and beckoned me to join in the chorus, simply because I recognized the melody. That was Daddy's song. It didn't mean it had to be mine.

I tossed and turned but I never fell asleep. At about 2:00 A.M. I got out of bed to use the bathroom.

I tried to go back to bed but my mind was in a twist. I felt like Daddy was speaking to me but I didn't know what he was trying to say. *What were the words under his words?*

History repeats itself over and over and over again. It's the natural course of life. Unless you force it to do otherwise. Unless you do something extreme.

I had to do more than *not* rob somebody if I wanted my life to turn out different.

I jumped up and looked at the clock. It was four o'clock Saturday morning. The bus had left for Austin Thursday with everyone on board for the state UIL competition. The preliminary poetry rounds were Friday night and I'd missed them. It was too late.

Or was it?

I am the master of my fate: I am the captain of my soul.

I wasn't sure what it all meant to me anymore. Up until that point I'd mainly been thinking of the money I might win. But I also wanted to overcome my fear, to prove to myself that I really was different from Daddy. And then there was the thing Suzie had said about my words giving people hope.

I wanted to rush into Mama's bedroom and wake her up, but I didn't dare. I wanted to tell her, *There are things you can believe in.*

Believe in me, Mama.

Believe in me . . . Please . . . Just once.

I hurried to the kitchen. Mrs. Peterson had given all of us an announcement telling us where the events for the state meet were scheduled. I had hung it on the refrigerator with a magnet, but now I couldn't find it.

All I could remember was that the competitions were to be held at the University of Texas campus. I had no idea where that was. I remembered vaguely that if I drove to San

Antonio I could catch the interstate to Austin. Surely there would be signs to the university. But that meant three hours of driving on the interstate. All I had was a hardship license and I didn't even carry auto insurance.

I got dressed and sneaked out past Jake, who was asleep on the couch. I went back to the café and took the keys sitting next to the register.

I felt guilty about leaving Mama. I couldn't just run off and leave her with Daddy freshly dead and not even buried. He'd asked me to take care of her with his last, dying breath.

But he'd also made me promise to take care of myself.

I grabbed a paper napkin and scratched out a note. *Mama, I've gone to Austin. Something I gotta do. I'll be back tonight. I promise. Love Kenny.* I meant those words. I was tired of running.

I grabbed the truck keys and ran out the door.

Finding the university was easy. Finding a place to park was another matter. I was surprised that there were so many cars at seven o'clock in the morning on a Saturday. I finally found a little neighborhood a few blocks from the university and walked, or rather ran.

The place was massive. It was much bigger than Southwest Texas State in San Marcos. In fact, it was bigger than the entire town of Comfort. I walked for half an hour, expecting to see some sign of the competition or at least some high school kids walking around. I finally stopped a couple of girls and asked for help.

"Do you know where the UIL competition is being held?"

They giggled and said something in French. They didn't even speak English. I stopped a man on a bike, but he didn't know what I was talking about either. I finally found a security guard. He gave me directions to the Thompson Conference Center.

I walked for another fifteen minutes before I realized I'd lost my bearings and was hopelessly lost. It was eight o'clock in the morning. I hadn't eaten breakfast. I didn't even know if the poetry competition was going on or if I'd missed it.

"Kenny," I heard someone call. I looked up to see Suzie running toward me. "I was afraid you weren't coming."

"Me too," I told her. "What are you doing here?"

"I came to watch you and take pictures for the yearbook. I heard about your dad. I was afraid you wouldn't make it, but I was hoping you would." She squeezed my hand.

I squeezed her hand back. *How could I ever have found her ugly?* We were cut from the same cloth.

"You're lucky," she told me as she led me down a long corridor in the Thompson Conference Center. "We lost the electricity last night and they couldn't hold the preliminary rounds. They're doing them right now."

She took me to a large lecture room. I'd never seen anything like it. It looked like it could seat three hundred people or more and most of the seats were filled.

Suzie and I had stood at the back against the wall. As I

looked at all those people, a brand-new wave of fear swept over me. What if I couldn't get up there?

"You're just in time," Suzie said. A girl stood up on stage reciting "Success is Counted Sweetest" by Emily Dickinson:

> *Success is Counted Sweetest*
> *By those who ne'er succeed.*
> *To comprehend a nectar*
> *Requires sorest need.*

I thought about Mama and Daddy and all their dreams forever just beyond their grasp. I felt tears welling up inside of me. Nobody said a word as the girl finished the poem. Suzie just squeezed my hand. When the poem was over no one applauded. I knew it was against the rules, but it felt weird with such a big audience watching. The girl who was reading walked to the back of the lecture hall and stood a few feet away from us.

Mrs. Peterson got up from her seat, came to the back, and hugged me. "You okay?" she asked softly.

"I'm all right," I lied. I knew everybody from Comfort had already heard about my daddy.

"You want to go on?" she asked.

I thought about how scared I was. I thought about how humiliated I'd be if I had to run off the stage in the middle of my reading. Then I thought about how I'd hate myself if I didn't take this chance. Somehow I had to pull through.

"Yes, ma'am," I said. "I want to go on."

"All right, then." She smiled. "They're doing the Diversity and the Human Experience category. Two more people and you're up."

A boy walked up and stood in front of the crowd, opened his black notebook, and started reading.

I turned to Mrs. Peterson in a panic. "I forgot my notebook!"

A crease spread across her forehead, then she smiled. "Don't worry about it."

She walked over and whispered something to the girl who had just finished reciting the Emily Dickinson poem. The girl nodded her head and lent Mrs. Peterson her notebook. Mrs. Peterson walked back over and handed it to me. "You're all set."

Then I heard my name called. "Kenny Willson."

I walked up to the stage carrying my borrowed poems. I stood up at the podium, looked out at the crowd, and froze.

There were a lot more people there than I'd been able to see from the back, and they were all staring at me. I realized I must have looked a fright. I hadn't slept. My hair was a mess. My clothes were wrinkled. I wondered if that's how Daddy felt when he had to sing in front of that crowd in Kerrville.

Maybe it was impossible to go around fear. Maybe the only way was through it. Walking through it, pushing through it, until you got to the other side.

"This one's for you, Daddy," I said, taking a deep breath. Then I started my introduction. "William Ernest Henley, Maya Angelou, Naomi Shihab Nye . . . what do these poets have in common? What do any of us have in common? Diverse, yet all the same. We breathe the same air. We bleed the same red blood. We dream the same dreams of freedom and of hope. And in the end we are all saved by simple acts of kindness." I looked up through the crowd at Suzie and Mrs. Peterson and the girl who had lent me her folder. I said, " 'Kindness' by Naomi Shibab Nye." Then I opened the black notebook and pretended to read, though the poem was in my head, not on the page.

> *Before you know what kindness really is*
> *you must lose things,*
> *feel the future dissolve in a moment*
> *like salt in weakened broth.*
> *What you held in your hand,*
> *what you counted and carefully saved,*
> *all this must go so you know*
> *how desolate the landscape can be*
> *between the regions of kindness.*
> *How you ride and ride*

thinking the bus will never stop,
the passengers eating maize and chicken
will stare out the window forever.

Before you learn the tender gravity of kindness,
you must travel where the Indian in a white
    poncho
lies dead by the side of the road.
You must see how this could be you,
how he too was someone
who journeyed through the night with plans
and the simple breath that kept him alive.

Before you know kindness as the deepest thing
    inside,
you must know sorrow as the other deepest
    thing.
You must wake up with sorrow.
You must speak to it till your voice
catches the thread of all sorrows
and you see the size of the cloth.
Then it is only kindness that makes sense
    anymore,
only kindness that ties your shoes
and sends you out into the day to mail letters
    and purchase bread,

> only kindness that raises its head
> from the crowd of the world to say
> It is I you have been looking for,
> and then goes with you everywhere
> like a shadow or a friend.

When I was done I returned the notebook and thanked the girl who had loaned it to me. Then I went with Mrs. Peterson and Suzie back to the hotel and for the first time in over forty-eight hours, I slept.

chapter 21

Mrs. Peterson woke me up at two-thirty that afternoon. "You made it to the final round," she said excitedly.

"And we've been shopping," smiled Suzie.

Mrs. Peterson laid a new pair of pants and shirt on the foot of the bed. "I hope they fit. You'd better hurry up and get dressed. The competition is in one hour." With that she hurried out.

"I have something for you too," said Suzie. She handed me a black notebook. I held it up to my nose, taking in the beautiful aroma of genuine leather.

Suzie didn't ask what I was doing. She just smiled.

I opened the notebook to find a pad of blank paper and a pen inside. I didn't know what to say. I couldn't remember the last time anybody gave me a real gift.

"Thanks," I whispered.

"It's for today, but it's also for tomorrow. For all the new poems you're going to write." She started to leave, but she paused at the door and turned back toward me. "It's *your* poem you oughta be reciting," she told me.

She took me off guard. "Mine isn't as good as the others," I stammered.

Then she gave me a look that unsettled me. She seemed to see into me, through me, past me, to my better self. "But Kenny, it's *yours*. That's what makes it what it is."

———

At three-thirty we were back in the same lecture room at the Thompson Conference Center, but this time every seat was filled and people were standing all along the back wall. Fortunately, we'd arrived early enough to get seats in the front row. There were six finalists and I was the last to perform. I broke out in a sweat before the first reader was done and I kept sweating until it was my turn to read. I'd never perspired that much. Not even during two-a-day workouts for football. I wondered if this was ever going to get any easier.

I walked up to the podium when they called my name, gave my introduction for my Words of Inspiration poems, and recited my selections by Frost and Shakespeare. Then I did something I'd never dared to do before. I looked out at the audience. They were on the edges of their seats, leaning toward me. Listening to me. *Me*. A scrawny kid from Comfort, Texas. I looked back at the empty pad in my notebook and realized that the future was a blank page. Anything was possible. I recited the Byron poem and then I was done. But I couldn't bring myself to step down off the platform. I knew I still had a good two minutes before the seven-minute time limit was up. I looked back down again at the white page and suddenly I realized that this was what I was born to do. I was afraid I might get disqualified but it didn't matter. I looked out at the audience and said, " 'I Ain't Goin' Down,' an original poem by Kenny Willson."

There were some murmurs as the judges turned and spoke to each other but I went on anyway. I was tired of swallowing my words. I needed to speak them:

> *I ain't goin' down, Mama,*
> *I ain't goin' down.*

I thought of all the times I'd bitten my lip and buried my feelings. I could no longer hold them back, nor did I want to.

> *You can lock me up in your Coke can house,*
> *'Til I'm busting at the seams.*
> *You can whoop me like a dog*
> *While I listen to your schemes.*
> *You can take away my pride.*
> *You can pull me off the team.*
> *You can step on me 'til I squirt blood,*
> *But you ain't taking my dreams.*

It's funny how words sound different when you speak them from the way you imagine them when they're just floating around in your head.

I ain't goin' down, Mama.
I ain't goin' down.
You can cook me in a vat of grease,
You can drag me through the town.
I can't do nothin' to appease.
You still think I'm lowdown.
If it helps your troubled mind to ease,
Then I will be your clown.
But your Jack shack flack can't hold me back.
Though you pin me to the rack.
For one day soon, I will rise.
I'll mobilize before your eyes.
Your schemes and extremes I'll neutralize.
'Cause I ain't goin' down, Mama.
I ain't goin' down.

I stopped talking and nobody said a word. From where I was standing it appeared that nobody even breathed.

Then, from the far back of the room, someone I recognized stepped forward. It was Mama.

My heart seemed to stop beating.

Her eyes were ablaze. She looked like somebody who had just found a lost toddler and didn't know whether to hug it or scream at it. She looked small and insignificant as if she'd shrunk three sizes.

Then Jake, who had been standing next to her, stepped

forward and started to clap. Then the whole room burst out in applause, all except Mama.

I looked out into the crowd. I could name the people who cared for me. Mrs. Peterson, Dr. Adams, Francesca, Jake, and Suzie Blackwell. Mama might kill me, but I didn't care.

The crowd gradually thinned. Suzie and Mrs. Peterson walked up on the stage and hugged me. Everyone was heading over to the LBJ Presidential Library next door for the awards ceremony. I told Suzie and Mrs. Peterson to go on without me. I'd meet them later.

Then there was just me and Mama. She walked down the aisle toward the stage, clutching the UIL announcement in her hand. She'd been crying. She stood below, looking up at me and said, "I guess you don't think too highly of me."

I wasn't fearful. I wasn't even angry. I'd opened the gate but anger hadn't consumed me. My courage had consumed my fury. I didn't feel rage for Mama. All I felt was pity. "Mama," I said. "I don't want to fight you anymore. You're too strong. I need you on my side."

I walked down off the stage and opened my arms in truce, not sure if she'd hug me or whack me or just turn away and ignore me. She folded into my arms and it was as if we'd suddenly exchanged places. As if I was the parent and she was a little child.

"You done all right, Kenny," she said.

Then we both cried.

I'd never been in a place like the LBJ Library. Thick red carpet covered the floor and dark wooden shelves lined the walls clear up to the ceiling. When they announced the poetry-interpretation category, we six finalists walked down the long aisle to a row of steps.

There was so much more spoken in the intense silence of this audience than in all the cheers and hollers of the football stadium crowd.

I felt like I was floating, being carried on the shoulders of Henley, Frost, Angelou, Nye, and a host of others. As I stood on the steps, looking out at the audience, with Mrs. Peterson standing behind me, I knew I had found my tribe. I had found my team.

I took my first-place medal and put it in a shiny, clean Crisco can along with the letter from the University Interscholastic League encouraging me to apply for a list of scholarships when I got ready to go to college. I put the Crisco can under the bed where my money box used to sit. I knew Mama wouldn't look there. She had a knack for not looking into things she didn't want to see. She never hit me again, but she never entirely quit being Mama either. When the pressure around the café started getting to me, I'd open the can and run my fingers over the letters inscribed on the medal.

I took three summer classes that year and when school

started back in the fall, Mama let me join the football team and the band again. She decided to turn the café into a pancake house and hired some help.

I stayed on the school paper and signed up for the UIL again.

Suzie Blackwell and I got to be pretty good friends. As it turned out, she and I had much more in common than Cindy and I ever did.

One night Suzie and I were sitting out behind the café on the milk crates looking at the stars. Roy junior was asleep on my lap. He'd been sticking to me like a shadow and I'd let him. One day he would be able to look out into a crowd and name the people who cared for him. I wanted him to see my face among them.

Suzie told me how Cindy had cried for a week, having just found out she was pregnant again. "What makes people do the same stupid things over and over again?"

"Comfort," I said. "They gravitate to what's familiar, even if it's painful."

"Comfort?" she said, then she nodded in understanding.

That night long after the pancake house closed and Mama and Roy junior were sleeping I sneaked into the café and played Daddy's tape:

> *Misery's at my shoulder,*
> *Sorrow's my next of kin.*

But they've grown to be familiar,
So I think of them as friends.

I made a promise that night to my daddy.

"I will never choose familiarity over freedom," I said, "nor comfort over quest."

Then I sat down, opened my black leather notebook, and wrote a poem for my daddy. "Roy Dan Willson, the Best Dang Country-and-Western Singer That Ever Lived."

It was to be the first of many.

ABOUT THE UNIVERSITY
INTERSCHOLASTIC LEAGUE

Every effort has been made to portray an accurate picture of the UIL events; however, the UIL does not give cash prizes, nor does it allow its participants to be awarded cash prizes or other gifts by individuals or outside organizations. Also, a participant may recite only *published* poems. Besides these two discrepancies, I believe the representation of the competition in my story is an accurate one.

Receiving a scholarship from one of the University Interscholastic League Foundation organizations was a deciding factor in my ability to acquire a university education. I applaud all youths that embark on these or any other such contests, no matter what the final outcome or placing.

Although all states participate in interscholastic competitions of some kind, the one in Texas is the most highly endowed. Since 1954 the University Interscholastic League Foundation has given out over twelve million dollars in scholarships. They have had a positive impact on the lives of more than twelve thousand Texas high school students. I am fortunate to have been one of them.

About Comfort, Texas

Comfort is a lovely little town located in the hill country of south central Texas at the junction of Cypress Creek and the Guadalupe River. It lies west of San Antonio and southeast of Kerrville where the famed Kerrville Folk Music Festival takes place every summer. The town was founded in 1845 by German intellectuals, "free-thinkers" who immigrated to Texas looking for a better way of life.

I chose "Comfort" as the title of my book simply because it so strongly reflected the theme of the novel. I knew nothing about the town when I began writing, so any similarities between the characters in my book and real people is strictly a coincidence. Upon completing my first draft, I made a visit to Comfort and found a delightful community with antique shops, bed and breakfast establishments, historic buildings, and lots of interesting German history. Kenny's desperate desire to leave Comfort is in no way a reflection on the real town, but rather an indicator of the limited choices of an entrapped youth.

ACKNOWLEDGMENTS

I would like to thank my agent, George Nicholson, for his belief in *Comfort,* and my editor, Margaret Raymo, for leading me gently through the rewriting process. Also, I would not have been able to write the book without the help of my "in-house" editors, my husband, Tom, and my daughter, Kristen. Special thanks go to Jana Riggins of the University Interscholastic League for reading the final draft and giving me valuable information about the UIL poetry interpretation competition; Gary Oliphant, principal of Comfort High School, who provided important information about the school; and John and Melinda McCurdy, the owners of Brinkman House Bed and Breakfast, who showered my husband and me with wonderful hospitality and shared fascinating stories about the history of the town of Comfort.

I owe a debt of gratitude to those who read the manuscript in its neophyte stages: the members of my critique group, Robert Weber, Gloria Mallory, and April Kopp; as well as Paula Paul, who encouraged me to keep going after reading my first chapter. Finally, I would like to thank the University Interscholastic League for the tremendous difference they have made in the educational opportunities of so many Texas young people.